A BRIDE FOR DARRELL

The Proxy Brides Book #17

Marisa Masterson

A sweet, historical western romance in the Proxy Bride series...

If Darrell Dean wants to inherit half of the Silver Queen mine, he needs to marry. Though he doesn't even like the girl, he agrees to marry the local saloon owner's daughter. He doesn't expect the surprise that he receives when a woman interrupts the wedding.

If Willa VanDurring wants to escape the danger stalking her, she needs a new name and a somewhere far away to go. At her guardian's urging, she agrees to marry Darrell Dean by proxy and then immediately leaves to join him in Colorado. She doesn't expect to interrupt his wedding when she arrives.

Can a man who didn't agree to marry the proxy bride and a woman pursued by murderers make a life together? What happens when the danger finds her? In a town with no law, how will she survive?

TABLE OF CONTENTS

Dedication vii

Chapter 1 1

Chapter 2 28

Chapter 3 45

Chapter 4 63

Chapter 5 83

Chapter 6 95

Chapter 7 111

Chapter 8 129

Chapter 9 139

Chapter 10 159

Epilogue 167

Leave a Review 176

Sneak Peek 177

About Marisa... 197

Acknowledgments 199

DEDICATION

For Trevor, the life-long love God gave me.

CHAPTER 1

The bald-headed judge took the cigar out of his mouth and rested it on a convenient ashtray. Staring at Willa VanDurring, he drummed his fingers impatiently on the lawyer's desk and glared. "I'm due to try a case in twenty minutes. Where's your other witness?"

His brusqueness added to the man's air of importance. That along with Miss Blackthorn's secrecy and talk of witnesses heightened her already piqued curiosity and alarm.

Mr. Barrett, the lawyer she'd met minutes before, moved to the doorway of his office and called to his secretary. With that young man's arrival, the judge asked which person would stand as proxy and who would act as the witness. Though

Willa recognized the word proxy, she still fixed a confused gaze on her guardian.

Turning for help to the only person in the room she trusted, Willa asked, "Miss Blackthorn, why is a proxy needed?" Then she decided good manners could fly out the window. She needed to get to the heart of what was happening to her.

"What am I doing here?" Rather than ask that of the head mistress, she pinned Mr. Barrett with an intense stare. The man nervously pulled at his paper collar.

"Certainly, Miss VanDurring, I will be happy to explain." He was cut off by the shake of her guardian's head.

With a nervous fidget, the woman smoothed her black skirt and the story of the red-headed man and talk of danger spilled out. Willa learned a red-haired man with a scarred left cheek had loitered outside the school for the last week. Miss Blackthorn told her about Roger, the groundskeeper at Blackthorn's Academy, visiting a local tavern and hearing the man drunkenly mutter threats against Willa.

"I'm very worried Willa, concerned enough to push you into marriage to hide you away." She met her gaze directly, allowing Willa to see her fear as well as to hear it in her tone. Since she kept her emotions closely guarded, this impacted the young lady greatly and truly made the decision for her.

The entire time she spoke, short though it was, the judge tapped his fingers on the desk. The tension created by the impatient tapping along with Willa's trust in Miss Blackthorn led to a snap decision. Suddenly, the reason for a proxy became clear. She needed to disappear. At the urging of her trusted teacher and guardian to go along with the plan, she agreed to become a proxy bride.

Married to a stranger! With no warning and forethought, Willa committed herself to an unknown man named Darrell Anders Dean. Later, as she thought back on it while rocking endlessly on a train to Colorado, she realized her adventure actually started out, quite innocently, the day Aunt Rhoda arrived at the Academy in Rockland, New York.

"Miss Blackthorn wants to see you, Willow Tree."

She knew by Geneva Watson's smile she was in trouble. The girl disliked her, for whatever reason, and insisted on using that ridiculous nickname when she spoke to her. Today Geneva enjoyed her role as messenger of Willa's distress.

Willa shrugged. No matter how many times teachers chastised that it was not ladylike to shrug, she persisted in the habit. When she didn't say anything, Geneva snorted—also an unladylike practice—and flounced off.

The summons honestly surprised her. She searched her memory for a prank or misdemeanor the headmistress might have discovered. Nothing came to mind, increasing Willa's anxiety.

The students had received a free day before the start of the new term. She was spending that January day reading *Carmilla*, having smuggled it into her rooms last Saturday. She began reading it by candlelight last night but found the vampire character too scary right before going sleep. She had decided to ask the groundskeeper to buy something romantic next time.

At Miss Blackthorn's door, Willa touched her strawberry blonde hair, ensuring it hadn't escaped her bun. This was the first year she'd been allowed to put her hair up rather than leaving it lay in a braid down her back. She'd been given the honor since she'd turned eighteen two years prior. This year she would graduate, as Miss Blackthorn had declared she could think of nothing more to teach her in order to keep her at the school.

Thoughts of leaving brought tears to her eyes. Willa had been in this same school since the age of four. Though she'd been too young to attend Miss Blackthorn made an exception, thanks to her grandfather's money she was certain. Thus, she'd lived here, both school time and holidays, for the last fifteen years.

Smoothing out the skirt of her dress, she schooled her features into a serene expression and knocked on the door. As footfalls approached on the other side of the portal, she straightened her carriage, determined not to embarrass or disappoint

Miss Blackthorn by showing any hint of nervousness.

That lady opened the door wide and waited for Willa to enter. "Ah yes! Willa. Prompt as always."

Following behind her, she spoke to someone already in the room. "Here she is now, Miss VanDurring. I hope you'll be pleased by how well she's advanced."

Across the room, Willa spied an elegantly dressed woman seated before Miss Blackthorn's desk. The woman raised a quizzing glass and the feathers in her hat danced as she looked her up and down. Setting the glass aside, she gave Willa a tight-lipped smile.

"My yes, she's a lovely young woman. And such grace and poise." She looked toward Miss Blackthorn. "You and your teachers are to be congratulated."

When she turned back to Willa, she fixed what she must believe was a welcoming smile to her lips. At the time Willa wondered if she scowled more often than she smiled, as the expression appeared to take considerable effort. Still, she appreciated the attempt since smiles were rare at The Blackthorn Academy for Young Ladies.

"Willa, I've found you. I'm sorry it's taken years, but here I am now to take you home." She offered no explanation or introduction and Willa was flabbergasted by the bluntness of her declaration.

She waited for her to say something so Willa quietly said, "Thank you, Mrs.--?"

Giving a rusty laugh, she introduced herself. "Of course, I shouldn't have expected you to recognize me. It's been fifteen years, after all. I'm Aunt Rhoda." Then she paused, obviously expecting the name to mean something to her.

When Willa didn't say anything, she continued. "You don't remember me? I'm your father's sister, God rest his soul, and you lived with me before going to school."

Here Willa raised a brow in question. "Miss Blackthorn told me I lived with my grandfather prior to coming here." She let the statement hang in the air.

The elegant lady gave a tight smile. "Yes, and I lived there as well. Father hid you away, for his own reasons you understand. I've tried to find you for years. I promised your dear mama, on her deathbed, to care for you. So here I am now to take you home with me."

Aunt Rhoda reached out and gripped her hand as she said that. She had been touched so rarely that this melted her fear as well as her heart. Willa wanted family and dreamed for years of someone coming to visit her here.

Looking to Miss Blackthorn, she asked, "Miss, am I to go with her?" The headmistress was the closest to a mother figure in her life so she sought guidance from her about this tremendous change.

The woman in question moved to sit behind her desk and stared at Aunt Rhoda. Miss Blackthorn spoke to her aunt instead of answering Willa's question directly. "You may be unaware of this, but I am Willa's guardian until she reaches the age of twenty or marries. She will not be leaving with you."

She wasn't being sent away. Blackthorn Academy had been her world and as well as her family. The head mistress's statement sent a flood of relief through Willa.

"I'm sorry Aunt Rhoda. Though I would be delighted to get to know you better, I cannot leave with you."

The previously congenial woman rose with a snarl. She flounced to the door. Before exiting she turned and shouted, "We shall see about that Willa!" Then she was gone, the short train of her gown and an atmosphere of tension trailing behind her.

Miss Blackthorn waved a hand to the chair where Willa's aunt previously sat and indicated she should occupy it. Willa sat and waited in silence for a few minutes while the head mistress steepled her hands and tapped her lips with her pointer fingers, deep in thought

When she finally spoke, the determination on her face told Willa her decision might prove momentous. "It is time, Willa, that you know more of your grandfather. I can't tell you the reason you were sent to me so many years ago. However, I can tell you that the man lies very close to death now. The lawyer has kept me informed of that as I send updates on your progress to him."

Though Willa's lips trembled a look of censure from her teacher had her quickly schooling her features as she had been taught. Grief, she'd learned, must be private. In control again, Willa asked emotionlessly, "Am I to go to my grandfather before he passes?"

A look of regret flitted with lightning speed across Miss Blackthorn's face before she mastered it. "No, I did not mean to imply that by sharing the information with you. I simply wanted you to understand that his passing might involve an inheritance. I fear your life will change drastically in the near future."

As if clairvoyant, Miss Blackthorn's words proved true. After a handful of days passed, Willa and her guardian journeyed by carriage to train depot. When asked where they were headed, the head mistress vaguely responded, "Let it be a surprise." What an understatement that proved to be!

They made a short trip by rail to the Grand Central Depot. There her guardian secured a cab. As Willa had only rarely been in Manhattan, she gawked with wonder at the buildings.

The cab dropped them in front of a narrow brick building not far from the New York City Courthouse, which Willa could see in the distance and recognized from a school trip. Miss Blackthorn didn't let her enjoy the sights though.

Miss Blackthorn hustled Willa into the brick building. Quickly reading the signage on the building, Willa saw it housed the law offices of Young, Young, and Barrett. A few minutes later, she learned it was Mr. Barrett who they had come to see.

Once inside the office, he invited them to sit in straight back chairs arranged at angles in front of a dark oak desk. Before he could speak, the door opened. Turning to look behind her at the door, she saw an older, balding man with mutton-chop side burns scowling in the attorney's direction.

"I'm due to try a case in twenty minutes. Where's your other witness?" And that began the wedding.

So, she found herself married by proxy to one Darrell Anders Dean.

Mr. Barrett folded the marriage license as well as another piece of paper and placed them in an envelope. He held it out to Willa. When she grasped it, he refused to release the envelope until receiving her promise to guard it and deliver it to her husband.

Husband! What had she done?

Miss Blackthorn hurried her out of the office and into another cab. Back at the Grand Central Depot, she purchased tickets for them but with separate destinations. Willa did not return to the only home she could remember.

In the matter of a day, she found herself married to a stranger and on a train traveling west—

during January, no less! Once, heavy snow on the line halted them. Otherwise the trip was continuous. She slept on the train, stretching out on a row of seats when the train's lack of passengers allowed this.

When she snoozed, she dreamed of the red-haired man catching her. Awake, she gazed out the window at the snow-covered landscape and wondered about the man who ordered a bride. Soon, she would know whether Darrell Dean's hair was dark or blonde.

Why did he need a proxy bride? She hoped to learn the answer to that as well.

Willa supposed his hair color didn't matter. After all, she only needed a kind man and a safe place to live. Silver Town, Colorado was far enough away from New York, her former guardian assured her, that she would escape any danger pursuing her.

Why does the red-haired man chase me? Will my husband be kind?

Fear at the possible answers threatened to fill her. So far, her natural optimism helped keep that fear at bay. Now, being close to meeting my husband resurrected terrible scenarios in her mind.

Mr. Barrett assured her Mr. Dean was respectable, honorable, and not too old. Willa also knew him to be twenty-four, young to hold a respected position in the community. In his letter requesting a bride, he'd written that he needed a lady of grace and charm to assume the role of wife and hostess.

During her years at school, she rarely socialized so Willa failed to see why the attorney would select her as the bride for this man. When she'd tried to object that day, the judge's tapping fingers and Miss Blackthorn's frown quashed her protests and the wedding had proceeded.

"Silver Town's the next stop, Mrs. Dean. You're fortunate to come this year and not last. The new Willow Creek Canyon Depot just opened so you're right above Silver Town when we stop. Yes, ma'am, 1893 is shaping up to be a much better year for Silver Town than last year."

This conductor who traveled with her on the long journey from Chicago, where Willa had been required to switch trains, proved to be a great help. With his advice, she purchased box lunches and knew which depots were best for stretching her limbs.

Even with his recommendations, she disembarked at depots hesitantly. Miss Blackthorn's warning about the red-haired man with a scarred left cheek haunted her.

Why is the man after me? Why did Miss Blackthorn make me leave so quickly?

The conductor's words about Silver Town brought a sigh of relief to her. She longed to be held in her husband's protective arms with his dark head bent over her. *No, maybe it was a blonde head.*

The train came to a complete stop, bringing her back to the present. She picked up the carpetbag resting next to her on the seat and walked down the aisle to the door of the train car.

The carpetbag along with the trunk containing her belongings had been another of her guardian's surprises. Willa still found it hard to believe that Miss Blackthorn could so quickly pack her things. She'd been in class for only a short time that day.

Willa waited on the platform of the railway carriage. The conductor positioned a set of short steps and held up his hand. Descending, she thanked him warmly and walked a short distance away from the train, out of the way of other passengers. Then she stopped to look around.

Snow covered mountains swallowed Willa. Their majesty inspired awe in her but also fear as the landscape appeared alien considering what she'd always known.

What would the mountains look like in the spring when everything was green again?

At some of the train's previous stops, people held boards or paper with names written on them. Since Mr. Barrett assured her a telegram would inform Mr. Dean of her travel plans, Willa imagined a handsome man holding a sign with her name once she arrived at this stop. Looking around, she felt disappointed.

No one waited for her. Willa conquered her disappointment and decided she needed to find her trunk and then her husband in that order. Stiffening her spine and coaching herself not to worry, she located the station master and asked for help in claiming it.

Giving the station master the ticket, she escaped some of the wind by hugging a wall of the depot's small office. Tying the red woolen scarf more tightly at her neck and huddled more deeply into her black wool cloak, she watched for a man around Darrell Dean's age to make an appearance.

The station master returned before her husband appeared. "Where you headed ma'am? You want the trunk loaded on the wagon and taken to the hotel in Silver Town?" He looked at her expectantly, waiting for an answer.

"To tell the truth, I'm not sure what to do. I expected to be met by my husband, Darrell Dean."

Shock flashed across the station master's face.

"Ma'am, you need to get on the wagon. My boy's the driver, and I'll tell him where to take you. Don't worry." He hustled over to his son and yanked on the young man's arm. Then he hurried Willa aboard the wagon.

The trip from Willow Creek Canyon to Silver Town plunged downhill. The steepness caused her to hold her breath. Willa feared, at any moment, the wagon might plummet to the valley below.

She wanted to ask the young man where his father said to take her. On the other hand, she didn't want to distract him. So instead, Willa held her breath, both out of fear and so she didn't chatter nervously.

We arrived at the edge of a collection of tin and wooden buildings she assumed formed the town. The wagon stopped in front of an unpainted wooden church. A sign outside proclaimed it the Silver Town Community Church.

Why did he stop here?

The young man hustled her down. "Best hurry up those steps ma'am and stop the doings." His command confused her, having no idea what the doings he spoke could be.

"Will I find my husband inside?" The young man bobbed his head and made a shooing motion with his hands.

"Don't worry 'bout your trunk. Just get on in there as quick as you can." His look of near panic further confused her. It also sent a frisson of fear traveling down her spine so she rushed up the steps, raising her skirts slightly to do so.

Opening the church door, she slipped inside. The words Willa heard clarified the station master's concern and the boy's panic.

"And do you, Darrell Anders Dean, take this woman to be—"

Forgetting the polite manners which she'd been taught, she screamed, "Noooo!" cutting the pastor off in mid-sentence. Faces turned her way, some showing anger while others had curiosity stamped on them.

The Pastor's booming voice echoed in the church, with anger clearly evident in his tone. "Young woman, why are disturbing a sacred occasion?"

A big man with a brocade vest and black suit leapt up from the front row and stormed toward her. His face reddened more deeply with each step. She would swear she actually heard him snort and growl as he approached.

A man with oily, pomaded dark hair followed behind him. Oddly enough, that man wore a grin of triumph as he looked at her.

Once the big man halted almost in front of her, he roared, "Get out! We don't want your kind in here." Willa wasn't sure what kind he thought she was.

Willa stilled her trembling at the man's approach. He frightened her so that she wasn't able to utter a word. Standing in front of her, he blocked the path and kept her from reaching the pastor to explain. She couldn't even get a good look at her husband, the man standing at the altar with another woman!

Mentally coached herself to be calm, she stammered out, "I can't leave without my husband." Then she held her hands out beseechingly.

"Well woman, who's your husband?" At last the big man was giving her a chance to speak.

She took a breath to steady herself and said in a low voice, "Darrell Anders Dean."

A scream from the altar reverberated through the small church. Looking around the big man's shoulder, she watched the bride crumple and fall. The dark-haired groom looked down at her and then at Willa. In that moment, she saw him for the first time.

His impassive face appeared to have been carved out of stone. Still, she appreciated his chocolate brown hair and his nicely cut frock coat stretched across magnificently built shoulders. He appeared to be someone who could definitely protect her from the red-haired man.

The moment seemed frozen in time. Willa looked at him with admiration. He looked at her expressionlessly, with one dark eyebrow raised.

Then he motioned her forward with a crook of his finger.

Though she tried to move around the big man, he refused to budge, glaring at her like a dog in a fight over his favorite bone. When the groom realized she couldn't reach him, he calmly stepped over the bride, who still enjoyed her swoon, and walked down the aisle of the church.

"Murphy, move out of my way!" Darrell's baritone voice curled her toes, regardless of its commanding tone. Silly romantic that she knew herself to be, she imagined what sweet words said with that voice would do to her insides.

The big man, Murphy she assumed, refused to move. Instead he turned his glare on the groom. "What are you trying to pull over on my daughter, you no good—"

Curse words started and she quickly put her hands over her ears. She'd been instructed at school to do that, if ever caught in such a situation. Willa watched and didn't remove her hands until she saw Darrell's lips moving.

"—no idea who this is. Wouldn't I remember a wife?" He shoved Murphy and this time the man gave ground. Once he moved out of the way, Darrell walked directly to her.

"Miss, I'll be honest. I can't remember ever meeting you." Here he paused, probably to find out what she'd say.

When she merely gave an unladylike shrug, he went on. "Don't you care that I don't remember you?"

Willa shook my head. "No, because we haven't met yet. Though, I am surprised you don't remember the arrangements you made."

"And what would those be ma'am?" Skepticism replaced his impassive look; it was easily discerned on his previously emotionless face.

"Why, for a proxy bride, sir. Certainly, you remember!" At that comment, another shriek rose from the direction of the altar.

Murphy left them and headed to the front of the church. "I hope he's going to comfort that poor girl!"

"Never mind her. You say we married by proxy. Do you have papers to prove this?" Darrell dismissed the woman he almost married.

What kind of a man could be so callous?

"Yes, of course I do. Mr. Barrett of Young, Young and Barrett gave me an envelope of papers to deliver to you." She smiled at him, pasting on a look that she hoped expressed confidence. Now that they were discussing the facts of the marriage, Willa felt on firmer footing, so to speak.

He held out his hand. Probably for the papers, she believed.

She shook her head in return. "I really don't think this is the time or place for this discussion. Couldn't we go to your home or someplace more private?"

Raising one eyebrow, Darrell's dark eyes bored into hers as if to assess her intent. Then with a short nod, he walked around her.

At the door of the church, he turned and said, "Well, aren't you coming?" Without waiting for Willa, he let himself out the door.

Callous and rude! Why hadn't he taken her arm? The attorney described him as respectable. So far, she had doubts in that regard.

Still, I'd pledged myself to him. I needed to demonstrate how agreeable I could be before he gets to know the real me.

After he left, she felt like a curtain rose on a stage production. The wilted bride who had been softly crying while her father hugged her to his side pushed away from him. She straightened up and, with hands on hips, glared in Willa's direction. At the same time the strange man with the pomaded hair stared at Willa with a grin of triumph on his face.

Then the battle started. The bride screamed obscenities. After her sheltered life at the academy, Willa didn't recognize all the words she hurled. However, she did know slut and home wrecker. Breathing deeply and slowly to control anger at the woman's cattiness she moved to the door of the church.

Once there, she couldn't resist firing a parting shot. "I wasn't the one who tried to marry someone else's husband!" With that, Willa softly closed the church door behind her, showing grace and decorum by not slamming it.

To her dismay, she discovered the groom was nowhere to be seen. *Why didn't the man wait for me? What am I supposed to do now?*

Snow crunched under her boots as she walked. An odd white dog with eyes pointing in different directions yipped at her heels while attempting to wag his tightly curled tail. Ignoring him, she headed toward the collection of buildings.

After she'd taken a few steps, a whistle pierced the air.

"Hey, Miss Whoever-You-Are, you're going the wrong way." Standing at the side of the church, he motioned her over before returning to wherever he'd hidden.

Making her way around the corner of the church, Willa saw him stow away a blanket, guessing it had covered the horse hitched to a black carriage. When she reached the carriage, Willa waited for him to help her up.

And waited while he sat in the carriage, watching her. *Insufferable lout!*

Lifting her skirts, she gracelessly lumbered into the vehicle. This was an inauspicious beginning for their marriage to be sure!

Things could only get better from here.

CHAPTER 2

Could things get any worse? At issue were the Silver Queen mine and perhaps the continued existence of the town. Darrell told himself to keep that in mind.

True, he hadn't particularly wanted to marry Marie so he didn't feel disappointment at having the wedding stopped. Losing the money Big Murphy promised as a dowry didn't even bother him. None of that was important.

His focus centered on the Silver Queen. Inheriting it depended on marrying, crazy as that was. If he could believe this stranger's news, he'd already accomplished that. She arrived signed, sealed and delivered, so to speak. Trouble was, he didn't know if he could trust what she told him.

And, giving her a side-long glance, he knew he urgently desired to trust she was indeed his wife.

Nearly twenty-five and a healthy red-blooded male with all of the accompanying desires, Darrell supposed he should have already married again. During the nights, especially the cold ones, he got lonely and entertained the idea of marrying. Business kept his days so busy that he easily put thoughts of a wife and children clean out of his mind.

Still, Darrell put off marrying since he wanted the mercantile running well. Like many other businesses in town, the fire last year destroyed his store and inventory. He'd been hard pressed to recover financially, as well as physically.

Marie Murphy had persisted, though. She began visiting his store daily for one or two items. If customers crowded the mercantile, she audaciously put on an apron and pretended she worked there, helping to retrieve items shelved behind the counter. No matter how many times he reminded her to stay out of that area, she still went back there.

In addition to finding Marie irritating, her father didn't like him. Once he told Darrell he couldn't trust any man who refused to drink alcohol. Each time they met, Murphy glowered and muttered words like snob and prude.

No matter her father's opinion, she refused to leave him alone. She hinted to him about church socials and dances. The woman even had the nerve to let Darrell know the amount her father, a local saloon owner, offered as her dowry. Then she set his back up by looking around the store and, with a speculative gleam in her eyes, sneering "I can see the money would help a lot here."

Though they might have come close to marrying, it had been easy for him to ignore all her attempts to win his attention. Her type of woman didn't catch his eye. With her bright red hair and short, thin body, she seemed like a short elf rather than his idea of the future Mrs. Dean.

Now the woman next to him satisfied his every requirement for a wife, physically at least. With her shimmering red-gold hair and well-placed curves, she was no hardship to look at. If he did send a letter asking for a proxy bride—and just when would he have done that--he must have done a good job specifying the type of woman he wanted.

Could I have signed the proxy form and sent a request to the New York law firm during that lost week after the fire? Did I go through a proxy ceremony?

Folks in town said he'd been helping people right up to his collapse. He still had no memory of the time immediately after the fire.

According to those who lived in town then, he behaved quite heroically. Odd that he did so many things yet had no memory of them.

During their short ride into town, the woman's silence surprised him. His mother and sisters always chattered, as if they hated silence. This woman, evidently, wouldn't be the first to break the stillness between them.

"About the wedding you saw…" He wanted to explain that convenience rather than affection had him almost married to Marie. She cut him off before he could continue.

"I'm sorry if you're sad not to marry that woman, but I think you're better off with me." She looked him in the eye when she spoke. No wilting violet here.

"You missed the show she put on after you left. I didn't even recognize some of the names she screamed at me."

No surprise that Marie turned mean. As a shop owner, Darrell overheard tales whispered between the few women in town when they shopped at the store. Between gossip he couldn't avoid hearing and her own pushiness, he believed Marie could become nasty.

"Yeah, you're probably right. 'Cept I don't know you so I can't say you're a better choice." He couldn't stop the grin that covered his face at what he said next, no matter how hard he worked at maintaining his stoic expression.

"I'd be happy later to let you prove you are." After delivering that comment, Darrell watched her reaction to his veiled suggestion. She looked confused.

Good! She's an innocent. He was relieved, believing she might not be escaping from a questionable profession after all.

I probably shouldn't be so happy about that her naivety. As a widower, he was no innocent. Still, before her response, he wondered if she was pregnant or a prostitute seeking a better life. After all, what else could drive a woman to marry an unknown groom?

Their arrival at the livery cut short possible conversation. He helped her down, ashamed now at refusing to help her into the carriage, and took her carpetbag. Pleasant warmth from her hand traveled up his arm, a physical affirmation of his attraction for her.

Presenting her with his arm, he guided her out of the livery and onto the snow-covered dirt streets to his store. She looked around curiously but not with condescension, he gladly noted.

Only a handful of years old, Silver Town remained a rough mining town. He didn't know about this girl, yet he suspected by her refined speech she was used to better than Silver Town offered.

Wanting her to see the store, Darrell stopped at the front door rather than taking her around to the stairs in the alley and up the stairs that led to the outside entrance for his rooms. Unlocking the door, with a flourish of his arm he allowed her to proceed him into the one room mercantile.

Looking around, he tried to imagine it through her eyes. Shelves lined every wall, even on each side of the two windows that sandwiched the door. A long counter ran almost the length of the store with some of his most expensive items as well as the most popular canned goods within easy reach behind it.

The woman—*I should ask her name*—looked around with interest. Then she turned to him. "Since you have a key, should I assume this is your business?"

So, she didn't know much about him. How did she happen to marry him?

Now that was a strange question.

He decided to examine the papers she spoke of before asking any of the questions burning hotly in his mind. "Yeah, all mine. You'll be ready tomorrow to help me in the store?" To be honest, he wasn't sure if he wanted her help. Really, he just wanted to know how willing she would be to do what he asked.

"Of course, though I have no experience. It will be a wonderful chance to meet people in my new town." Her generous lips smiled at him, an open and beautiful smile showing true happiness.

She hadn't smiled like that before and he realized it transformed her from a pretty woman to something else entirely. The smile robbed Darrell of breath, as if he'd taken a punch in the gut. She became gorgeous, literally breathtaking, when she smiled like that.

What does she think of me?

He tried to put the brakes on his thoughts as well as his very physical reaction to her. After all, he didn't know if her claims were real. And Harv Perkins had a stake in seeing Darrell didn't marry and claim the inheritance.

Could this be one of his shenanigans? Maybe this woman was an actress he'd hired.

He remembered the grin on Harv's face right after the woman arrived. He'd seen it as he followed Murphy down the aisle.

"Let's go up to my rooms. You can show me those papers." Fingers crossed, there would be something in the papers to indicate if she were being honest.

While still back east, he had studied law for a year. That had been when he courted and then married his wife. *No, my first wife.* He barely stopped himself from shaking his head ruefully at that thought.

Also, he'd assisted a lawyer while pursuing his studies, so he did possess some experience with legal documents. After his wife's sudden death, Darrell had realized he couldn't imagine spending life as a lawyer or staying in his small hometown near New York City so he abandoned the career. Now he hoped some of what he'd learned might prove handy when reading over the documents.

Enjoying the view of his *possible* wife's ankles, he allowed her to go up the stairs first. His mother had taught him that a gentleman should do that for a lady, in case she stumbled backward on the stairs because of her skirts. She waited for him on the small landing in front of the door to his rooms, at the top of the stairs.

Since he always locked the door to his store, he never bothered locking the door to these rooms. Darrell reached around her, enjoying her sweet scent, and opened the door to the very small apartment.

The kitchen and parlor were one room, with a south facing, curtain-less window providing weak light in the waning winter afternoon. A door on the far wall led into the only bedroom.

A table with two chairs and an arm chair by the potbellied stove were his only furnishings, except for the bed and wardrobe in the bedroom. She wouldn't enter that room until he'd studied those papers. Her nearness already tempted him greatly.

How can someone who rode days on a train still smell sweet?

Motioning to a chair at the table, he directed her to sit. "Let me have the envelope you mentioned." Darrell didn't ask her name as he had intended, afraid he'd look foolish if he did. It should be on the papers so why bother asking her.

Setting her carpetbag by the door so she could quickly grab it should he prove her story false, Darrell joined her at the table and picked up the slim white envelope she drew out of her reticule. With great care, he smoothed out the two documents and then set to studying them.

The first, a marriage certificate, declared Darrell Dean Anders joined in holy wedlock with one Willa Louise VanDurring. Now he knew her name. He mentally said it. Willa. He liked its exotic sound and believed that it fit the beautiful woman sitting across from him.

"So, our anniversary's January 23rd, huh? We've been married a week already." Looking to her for a response, he was disappointed. She merely nodded without commenting on the certificate or the wedding.

The second document, he guessed, must be the request for a proxy he supposedly sent. Probably the lawyer sent it back in case anyone challenged the validity of the proxy marriage. With interest, Darrell noted the date of the letter to be a few days after Silver Town's fire.

When he first took the envelope from her, he recognized the law firm whose information was printed on its upper corner. Old Avery, his father-in-law, had employed Mr. Barrett to manage his finances as well as write his will after he'd left Silver Town and returned east to live with his spinster sister. Did the address printed on the envelope as well as Mr. Barrett's signature as witness prove this proxy situation was valid?

The signature at the bottom of the letter held particular interest for him. Though shaky, he recognized it since he saw it each time he signed a document.

But I have no idea who wrote the letter! That had been done by a different hand.

Perhaps his signature was shaky because he'd signed this during those days after his head injury. A falling beam struck him as he rescued the Jones boy from the fire. Did the unsteadiness prove he sent away for a proxy bride soon after the injury? That still didn't answer the question of who drafted the letter.

Looking up, he saw Willa watching him. She didn't look triumphant or nervous. She simply wore a patient expression and seemed calm.

What incredible poise she has!

Before he could comment on the documents, several hard knocks on the front door of the store interrupted them. It wasn't unheard of for him to open the store after the posted hours since men worked both first and second shifts in the silver mines. Often one would need something after coming off of second shift, around nine in the evening.

Excusing himself, he descended the narrow stairway and went to a window to the left of the door. With the last of the fading sunlight, he groaned at the sight of Big Jim Murphy standing outside his store.

Oh bear scat! Why did it have to be that man?

He was still working his mind around the facts he'd learned. He didn't feel ready to speak with Murphy about whether he could still marry Marie.

Reluctantly, Darrell opened the door. Behind him, he heard the gentle step of Willa's feet on the stairs. She must be curious. He liked that since he believed curiosity to be the sign of an intelligent mind.

When he opened the door a crack, Murphy pushed on it and forced his way into the store. Knowing the brawny tavern owner's reputation as a brawler, he hurried to put the counter between them. As he moved behind it, he noticed that Willa stayed at the bottom of the stairs and only peeked into the store.

"Well, you've lost out now Dean! I'm not letting you hurt my girl again." Red faced as always Murphy roared his words as he glowered at him.

Since placating the man seemed the intelligent thing to do, he spoke in a soothing voice. "I'm sorry for her disappointment. I'll be by tomorrow to explain it all to her and to apologize."

Murphy smirked, "Won't do you any good." Darrell resisted the urge to yell that he'd never really wanted to marry Marie and had been dragged to the altar in a last-ditch attempt to win an inheritance.

"Soon as you left the church, Harvey Perkins begged me to marry her. She was already in a white dress so I forced her to take him. Preacher married 'em before the guests could leave the church."

By his smug grin, Murphy clearly expected Darrell to be angry or upset. Murphy loved to upset men enough to provoke them into taking a swing at him. The man often boasted about how many noses he'd broken.

When Darrell only shrugged and stared at the man impassively, Murphy scowled and headed to the door. The windows rattled as he slammed it behind him.

"One less thing to worry about. Good riddance! Now Marie won't be chasing me anymore." Locking the door behind Murphy, he walked over to Willa and took her hand.

Pulling her into the store he asked, "Shall I cut us some cheese from the wheel? We could have cheese and crackers for supper."

Willa nodded. "That's fine. Let's grab some beans. I'll set them to soaking for tomorrow's lunch."

Just like that, they entered into normal married life. He hadn't commented on the documents or declared that he believed her to be his wife. She didn't seem to be waiting for that though.

He recognized that she confidently believed in the truth of their marriage and didn't expect him to be anything other than accepting of it. Well, that was fine with Darrell, especially considering the intense draw to her he felt. They were married, and he was keeping her.

Grabbing a bottle of wine from under the counter, he followed her up the stairs. He planned to enjoy a meager wedding supper and then a bountiful wedding night. After all, he had planned to be married that day. One woman was as good as another.

CHAPTER 3

One man was definitely not the same as the other. Their wedding night proved this to Willa.

In the cab on the way to Grand Central Station, Miss Blackthorn explained to Willa that she wouldn't be safe from the red-haired man unless Darrell and she were fully married. Then she'd described what being fully married involved. Human anatomy had not been a part of the curriculum at the school so she quickly tutored her. *Oh my!*

She warned her that men were unable to control their roughness when in an intimate situation. Since the woman never married, Willa wondered how she learned her information. Regardless, Darrell's care demonstrated to her that he was a prince among men.

She awakened before him and stretched out the last of the sleepiness from her body. Then she encountered a leg. This touch brought a flood of memories and sensations from the previous night.

Even with as gentle as he'd been, the newness of this intimacy sent a shock through her. She felt her cheeks redden and threw herself from the bed. Hurriedly, Willa wiggled into the white shirt waist and brown skirt she'd carefully hung on the armoire's door the previous night, to remove wrinkles from them.

Now standing in his kitchen, she struggled to find coffee. He had no coffee beans, no grinder, and no coffee pot. Below her, he had a store filled with items so it couldn't be that he wasn't able to buy those things.

Why doesn't he have such ordinary items? Should I wake him to ask?

At the thought of going into the bedroom, heat swamped her cheeks. *Oh drat! If just thinking about it makes me blush, how will I face the man?*

I'll know soon. She heard his steps in the bedroom. Wanting to appear busy when he left the bedroom, Willa returned to searching the cupboards, rearranging items as she went so they were organized in a way she found more usable.

Behind her, Darrell approached on quiet steps. She squealed in surprise when a soft, ticklish kiss landed on the back of her bent neck.

He chuckled at her squeal. "Good morning wife. Can I help you find something?"

The playful man kissing her neck seemed very different from the stoical mask he represented to the world. With a huff, she turned to him. "Where is your coffee pot? I wanted to have a cup ready for you before you rose this morning."

At the shake of his head, she assumed he meant he didn't drink coffee. "Oh, are you not a coffee drinker? Can we get a pot for me? I do need my morning cup to face the day."

"So that's why I'm getting the cold shoulder." He chuckled before continuing. "And yes, I do drink coffee. Each morning I make a pot of coffee down in the store. Customers warm themselves with it while they shop, especially in winter. Makes them look around longer."

How clever! He'd impressed her with his organized store and now with his idea for selling more. The rude man she'd met yesterday had been replaced by a sweet, smart business man. It seemed Mr. Barrett made the right choice of grooms for her after all.

Thinking about Miss Blackthorn and the lawyer reminded her of the need to warn Darrell about the red-headed man. Last night they'd sat at the table and shared the scant supper by soft light, the lantern turned low. She meant to explain then, but the wine relaxed her mind and Darrell played with her fingers across the small table. Before she thought too much of it, they'd moved into the bedroom.

With a blush covering her face as she remembered that, Willa ducked her head to avoid looking at him. Coffee and breakfast came first. Perhaps they could talk after that.

"Let's go on down and get your coffee brewing. While it's a boiling, maybe you'd like to shop for the staples and such. You cook, right?"

His hopeful expression made her laugh. Some of the awkwardness between them evaporated. "Yes, I know how to cook and keep house. The head mistress included it as part of the curriculum at the academy I attended."

Darrell held the door open. "Wait on the landing so's I can go down first. If you trip, I want you falling onto me."

Again, she appreciated how differently he behaved from the man yesterday at the church. Less formal and stern. She sent up a silent prayer of thanks to the Lord for the husband she'd married sight unseen.

Passing her husband to exit the rooms, she gave him her first smile of the day. His answering smile ignited warmth in her stomach, almost as if he'd touched her.

How unusual!

Once he started the coffee brewing, they gathered items, filling a wooden box he pulled from a store room she had yet to see. Willa planned to spend the morning making bread so yeast and bread pans went into the box. He filled a large metal container with flour for her and put a lid on it, saying he'd send it up for her when she returned upstairs.

Send it up? What an odd thing to say!

Then he surprised her when he started oatmeal cooking on the potbellied stove in the store. What a treat to have her husband make breakfast!

With everything ready and the "shopping" complete for that day, they sat in chairs placed next to the stove. "For customers to warm themselves," he explained before he bowed his head and prayed. He'd done that last night too, before their supper.

How wonderful it is to be married to a god-fearing man! I can't thank the Lord enough for that.

While they ate, a silence settled between them. Darrell broke the quiet first, clearing his throat nervously. "Willa, I want you to know that I'm not a man who runs around with women."

What an odd statement! Where was this coming from?

"I have some experience because I was married once. Sarah was her name. Anyway, I just didn't want you to wonder." Though she hadn't wondered before, hearing he'd been married made her start wondering.

"When was this and what happened to her Darrell?" Willa didn't understand the fear she caught a hint of in her voice. Suddenly she struggled not to wring her hands. Instead she forced a practiced expression of calm to settle on her face.

"Oh at least six years ago, soon after I turned eighteen. I was working for a lawyer and studying law at the same time." Another new fact about her husband, he hadn't always been a shop owner. With his almost offhanded mention of how long his wife had been dead as well as his warmth toward her last night in bed, Willa felt assured that he must not still carry a torch for the woman.

After she made no response, he continued in a sort of wistful tone. "We were only married a few months when she cut her hand badly. The doctor stitched it up, but it got infected." Darrell stopped his retelling to shake his head sadly.

"No matter what he tried, the infection spread." Reaching over, Willa squeezed his hand.

"I'm sorry you lost her. I think, though, I'm glad to be here with you. So, thank you for taking the risk to marry again." She gave him a gentle smile she hoped would console him, and he squeezed her hand in return.

"Anyway, after that, New York state was the last place I wanted to be. Her father, Dan Avery, and her cousin, Harv Perkins, decided to come out to Colorado. They decided to try mining. I had some inheritance from my grandfather so I came along and started a store."

The name Dan Avery meant nothing to her. Harv Perkins, however, sounded like a name she should know.

"Didn't Mr. Murphy mention his name yesterday?" *Did his cousin by marriage horn in and steal his bride?*

"Yeah. Guess he's married to Marie now. Good luck to him. They deserve each other." He confused her by chuckling. Evidently, he wasn't disappointed about losing the woman.

"Maybe you saw Harv? Slicked back, kind of oily hair."

Nodding she said, "I think so. Did he have a sort of odd grin on his face?"

"Yep, that was him. A real conniver. His mining claim went bust so he works for the bank in town."

This surprised her. Should the bank owner consider someone described as a "conniver" trustworthy? It wasn't her concern so she turned the conversation back to Sarah.

"Do you still love Sarah?" She wanted to know if she was in competition with a ghost.

He smiled, sadly Willa thought. "She was my first love so I'll always have a spot in my heart for her, but she's been gone a long time now. Much, much longer than the time we actually had together. I'm ready to move on."

The tone of his voice changed from wistful to determined, and he looked at her, frowning. "Speaking of moving on, I think we need to be married."

She gave him a startled look since she knew he considered the marriage license valid.

"The proxy is fine. There's something I can't put my finger on that seems wrong though. Maybe it's just that I want to hear you say your vows and to be able to say mine to you."

Willa smiled at that. So, the stoical man she'd met yesterday had a tender, romantic side. This thought pleased her.

"Perhaps the pastor could marry us after the store closes? Actually, I'm a Methodist. Does Silver Town have a Methodist church?" She supposed it shouldn't matter.

The preacher, at the church Miss Blackthorn insisted her students attend, adamantly declared theirs to be the only faithful Christian sect. All other churches preached heresy he'd said more than once.

Darrell shook his head. "Nope, Silver Town is lucky to have the one church. The man's a good preacher."

She shrugged, silently deciding to hold off judgment until she'd heard a sermon from him. He had frightened her yesterday when he objected to her interruption.

A knock on the door interrupted them. They'd finished breakfast, or close enough to call it done, so she gathered up the dishes while Darrell opened the door to his first customer of the day.

After depositing dishes in the sink upstairs, she descended the steep stairs again with care and returned to the store. "Darrell, please, could I watch the store while you carry the flour up for me? I want to set a batch of bread rising." A man near the far wall sorted through woolen shirts so she didn't think tending the store would be too difficult.

Darrell shocked her by shaking his head. "Not now. Maybe you have some cleaning or unpacking to do? I'll be up in a few minutes with the flour." He turned his impassive, no-nonsense look in her direction.

She returned to the apartment and stripped the bed rather than making it. After searching through the chest of drawers, she discovered an empty drawer waiting for her and a set of clean sheets. These she used to remake the bed. If she didn't manage to retrieve her trunk today, she would need to launder the clothes worn on the trip there so she planned to wash the stained sheets along with them.

Hearing footsteps on the stairs, she left the bedroom and found Darrell in the kitchen sliding up a small door in the wall. She hadn't realized he had a dumbwaiter and felt quite impressed at her husband's cleverness in having installed one. Considering the steepness of the stairs, she rejoiced knowing she would not have to carry anything heavy up them. He removed the container of flour and box of supplies from the dumbwaiters cart and set them on the table.

Turning to her, he sent an apologetic smile her way and brought up what had happened a bit ago. "Willa, sorry 'bout not taking your help in the store. That man can't be trusted. Had to confront him before 'bout pocketing items."

She felt better knowing why he refused her offer of help. The feeling reminded her of what it felt like to suddenly breathe after holding her breath for a time. "I did have work to do up here. You were right husband." She smiled to assure him that she appreciated his apology, and he returned to work.

Before mixing up the bread, she set beans to cooking in a pot on the back of the small cook stove. Then taking the receipt for bread from her carpetbag, Willa mixed together the ingredients.

While kneading the dough, raised voices alarmed her. Wiping her hands on a kitchen towel, she made her way to the store.

A red-headed woman screamed at Darrell. *Perhaps my guardian should have warned me about a red-haired woman instead.* Stopping to ensure that her expression appeared calm, Willa left the stairs and entered the store.

"…sneaky and untrustworthy person in our community. I wonder what the ladies' guild will think when I ask them to stop shopping here." The woman's face flamed as red as her hair.

She actually spit as she yelled. *This must be what people call spitting mad.*

"Now Marie, I was as shocked as you were yesterday. All I can say is I'm sorry." He paused and held up his hands in a beseeching gesture.

"Still, ours wasn't a love match. We both have what we wanted since we're married, just not to each other." Darrell definitely didn't know how to pacify a woman if he thought those words would make her happy.

Well, so this red-faced woman was the foul-mouthed bride from the church yesterday. The red dress she wore made Willa think of the woman as walking fire.

Hearing he didn't love the woman pleased Willa even while she felt sorry for Darrell since he had to deal with her. Wanting to stay out of the disagreement, she hovered at the foot of the stairs, standing as quietly as possible. Still, Willa must have made some small noise because the woman turned in her direction.

"I will make it my business to see that you are not accepted into our community. Enjoy your husband since you won't have any friends." Another woman might have made that her parting comment and flounced out of the store. This one held her ground, though, and waited for a response.

Breathing deeply before answering, Willa chimed back with a sweet voice. "Thank you for your welcome. I'm sure I shall enjoy very much getting to know the women in my new town." Then she smiled. Heaping flaming coals on her enemy's head seemed the wisest response.

At that the woman finally gave the expected huff and exited the store. She didn't flounce though. She stomped to the door and slammed it, like her father had done the night before. Hearing whispers in a corner, for the first time Willa noticed two women looking through the sewing notions.

Walking over to them, she smiled. "I won't offer my hand since I was busy kneading bread upstairs, but I'm Willa Dean."

Both women returned the smile. Maybe Marie didn't have as much influence over the community as she thought.

The ladies, much older than herself, introduced themselves as Mrs. Potter and Miss Emerson. The three chatted about their sewing projects. That normalcy seemed to erase any lingering tension that had filled the store with Marie's tirade.

When Willa excused herself to return to the bread, Mrs. Potter stopped her with a hand on her arm. "I can assure you as the pastor's wife, you will be a most delightful addition to our community. I look forward to hosting a ladies' tea in your honor."

This reinforced Willa's earlier thought that Marie must be deluded to believe she had influence over these women. At least, she hoped the other ladies in Silver Town would be as friendly as these two.

"Oh, you're the pastor's wife! We're hoping to visit this evening. Though we were married, by proxy you understand, Mr. Dean and I would very much like to say our vows before your husband." The smile on her face died at the concerned expression clouding Mrs. Potter's own visage.

"My dear! That will be impossible. My husband received a telegram early this morning from Denver. Though it was a rush, he did manage to leave on a train carrying ore. They don't like passengers you know, but dear Mr. Owens was the engineer so he allowed Mr. Potter to travel with him."

She shook her head and confusion showed on her face. "Such an odd telegram! We didn't even know that Mr. Potter's dear sister had arrived in Denver. To learn that she lies at death's door is especially disturbing, you can well imagine!" Mrs. Potter sadly shook her head to punctuate her words.

Listening, Darrell interrupted then, "No matter Mrs. Potter. I am so very sorry about your sister-in-law and hope she recovers."

Willa hurriedly added her own reassurance. "We definitely understand. As we're already married, we can wait for your husband's return." Wishing the ladies good day, she returned upstairs.

She didn't know why the sudden telegram and the pastor's departure bothered her. Later, after living through the danger they would face, she could see why she should have been concerned.

So many things around her had been done in a hurry, it seemed. The hurried wedding. Her quick departure for Silver Town. Miss Blackthorn's advice to quickly consummate the marriage.

Perhaps the combination of those events caused her sense of unease that day. Willa stood deep in thought, worrying that she was missing some clue. Then a thought came to her.

"Rats! I forgot to tell Darrell to be on the lookout for a red head."

CHAPTER 4

If I never see that red head again, I'll be a happy man! It didn't matter that she'd screamed at him. Darrell was simply relieved he hadn't married her.

True, he'd badly wanted to inherit Avery's rights to the silver mine the man shared with Clancy Walters. He had until the last day of January to marry. If he didn't, the rights to the mine would pass to Harv Perkins. In retrospect Darrell couldn't believe he thought the mine would be worth marriage to Marie Murphy.

He still inherited and had dodged marriage to Marie. She'd been the only unmarried female in town who was about his age and wasn't a widow saddled with a small tribe of children or a saloon girl. The competition with Harv went to his head and he'd given into Marie's hints and constant presence in his store.

Some months ago, he'd received a letter from Mr. Barrett that informed him both of Avery's death and the conditions of inheriting half interest in the mine. Still, he had been busy both healing and rebuilding his store so he didn't act on finding a wife. During the last few months, Harv began to boast about stealing the inheritance from him.

Between his competitive comments and Marie's pursuit, Darrell eventually gave in. After all, he didn't remember sending for a proxy bride. This thought made him wonder why it took so long for the bride to arrive since the date of the letter indicated he'd sent for her 5 months ago.

According to the letter from Mr. Barrett, he would need to marry by the end of January, six months after Avery's death. It was just after Christmas, when only one month remained before the deadline's end, that he had made the decision. While she was in the store, pestering him as usual, Darrell told Marie, "You know I'd only be marrying you to inherit the mine."

Marie narrowed her eyes. Darrell thought those eyes held a sort of speculative gleam. Then she said, "I won't care."

"Okay, let's get married," he told her.

Oddly enough, she didn't try to hug or kiss him. She simply ran out of the store to trumpet her news to the townsfolk. Another month followed, which he spent being pestered about wedding details, before he found himself standing before Reverend Potter.

Thank the Lord Willa arrived when she did.

He'd gone to his wedding trying to keep disgust off his face. He didn't want to marry Marie and wasn't sure he could give her a wedding night, no matter what Marie expected. In retrospect he knew that wasn't fair to Marie. Nonetheless, she'd been so insistent on marrying him that he'd decided she would agree to whatever he proposed.

Marriage is a holy institution! He experienced a heavy weight in his gut at the thought of how he'd approached it. It also caused him to be doubly devoted in his determination to know his new wife better. He was committed to strengthening their marriage after its unusual beginning.

When Willa came to the bottom of the stairs and asked if he would leave the store to have lunch, Darrell was mightily tempted to put up the closed sign. The day had been busy, though, with what seemed like the entire population of Silver Town coming into the mercantile.

They were curious and mostly bought only one or two items. "They didn't limit their questions about my new bride to only one or two," he grumbled to myself.

Willa caught the sound of that grumble, evidently. "I didn't hear what you said, Darrell."

Shaking his head, he explained, "Have the habit of talking to myself. Sorry." Then he directed his comments to her earlier question. "Could you bring lunch down here and eat with me?"

With a nod, she went back up the stairs and began carrying bowls down. He felt badly when he watched her repeated trips up and down the steep stairs. Nevertheless, the need to get to know her better was driving him so he said nothing.

She placed two bowls already loaded with servings of beans and rice on the long counter in front of him and waited for Darrell to bless the food. He'd noticed her bow her head before breakfast and was glad to know she had the habit of praying.

After the prayer, he nodded toward the chairs by the fire. Each took a bowl and settled into the chairs.

This was their third meal together and already they were developing a routine. He was coming to believe that Willa would be a very easy woman to live with.

At that moment, no customers shopped in the store. He planned to take advantage of the quiet to ask about her background.

Why did I push her into intimacy without even getting to know her? He mentally chastised himself for giving into that intense desire for her.

That he'd pushed for a wedding night was another reason he'd told her that he'd never had relations outside of marriage. He'd been a bit ashamed this morning and had imagined she would think of him as some kind of tomcat.

Before he could ask questions, she broke the silence. "I forgot to warn you about the red-headed man."

"What?" It was all he could get out. Her statement stunned him. It was so random.

"Tell me what you mean," he demanded gently.

"It's kind of a long story. I'll try to shorten it." She took a deep breath and walked to the counter to set her still full bowl down. Returning to the chair, she sat again and faced her husband.

"I grew up in a school for girls. Nothing prestigious but still very nice, I think. Anyhow, no one ever came to visit and I stayed there on holidays. About two weeks ago that changed."

Willa paused in her story and looked down to the hands entwined in her lap. They relaxed slightly when she looked at them as if she were willing herself to remain calm, he thought. Then she looked into his face and continued with her tale.

"Anyway, Aunt Rhoda appeared at the school. I'd never met her or at least didn't remember meeting her. I might have, perhaps, as a much smaller child. She indicated I had. Regardless, I needed a place to live and she offered me a home."

Why did she need a home? Even though Darrell wondered this he didn't ask, not wanting to interrupt her story.

"She told me she'd just learned where I was. Her father, my grandfather, hid me away years before and wouldn't tell her where he'd sent me. Anyway, she wanted us to spend time together so we could truly become a family."

Darrell had a goal of learning about her background, and he was gathering information about her. With that in mind, he forced himself to keep from urging her to hurry along with her story. He wanted to know what she'd meant by the red-headed man. Even so, he stayed quiet and listened.

"My guardian, the head mistress of my school, refused to let Aunt Rhoda take me with her, something I didn't want to do anyhow. My aunt angrily left. I haven't heard from her again, but after that visit a man appeared outside the school."

At this, he couldn't stop from interrupting. "The red-headed man?"

She nodded. "According to the groundskeeper, he is. And the man has a horribly scarred left cheek." Looking at her hands, she continued in a whispered voice, "He even threatened me with harm."

Putting a finger under her chin, he gently raised her gaze to his own. Caressing her cheek, he promised, "I will look after you. If he finds you, you aren't alone." Then he asked her to tell him how she became his bride.

With a finger tapping her lips as if to help her remember, she started her story again. "Ten days or so ago--I lost track while riding the train you see—Miss Blackthorn hustled me out of the school. Except for fieldtrips or dances at the local military school, I never left the academy and certainly never went alone anywhere with my beloved head mistress. So, you can understand how excited I was to take the trip with her. Still, I thought it odd that she wouldn't tell me where we were headed."

Willa paused again, staring down at her hands "She took me to Manhattan. I'd been there, but only for a few rare school trips, so I wanted to look around. She grabbed my arm and hurried from the street into a building. Mr. Barrett's law office, as I learned once we were inside."

She stopped and looked at him. Confusion filled her face.

This, in turn, confused him and he couldn't keep from interrupting her. "But why were you there and how does this all lead to a red-haired man?" If pushing intimacy last night hadn't revealed his tendency toward impatience, she would see it now.

"I'm sorry Darrell, remembering confuses me. I want to put the events together and make sense of it. Why did Miss Blackthorn insist on marriage rather than sending me to my grandfather? Is my aunt really a threat? Was that why?"

With a shake of his head to indicate he couldn't help her understand those things her husband opened his mouth to urge her on with the story. The jangle of the bell above the door was an unwelcoming and startling interruption.

Already irritated by the interruption, seeing Harv Perkins enter sent anger hurrying through Darrell. *Why shouldn't he come? His new father-in-law and wife have already been here to complain.* This visit completed the trio.

Preemptively, he held up both of his hands to keep him from speaking. "You here because of Marie? Already told her I'm sorry."

Harv snickered. "Nah, just wanted to be sure you knew she and I got married. You might say, after last night, we're very married." The man leered as he said that.

Darrell wasn't about to share the same information with him. In fact, he grimaced at the man's coarse statement.

Based on what the disgusting man said next, he must have thought that grimace was a reaction to losing Marie. "Face it. You lost. I got the girl and the money. Maybe even the mine."

Prickles of unease crawled on the back of Darrell's neck. "Why would you get the silver mine? It wasn't a race to see who married first. And if it was, I got married in New York last week."

Again, Harv gave that awful snicker. "That right? Sure it's legal? It'd be too bad if'n you weren't really married?"

Something in Harv's tone and expression caused fear to lance through Darrell. Harv's smile screamed, "I know a secret." The man almost confessed to knowing something, he thought.

The skunk still had friends in New York City, the man's hometown. Could he have planned this proxy marriage as a ruse? Was Willa part of it?

Perhaps Willa's poise and perpetual calm hinted at acting abilities. Would a woman go as far as giving up her virtue to act out a part she'd been hired to do? That didn't make sense and Darrell shook his head to dismiss any doubt about Willa from his mind.

When Harv saw the shake of his head, the man grinned more broadly and picked up the topic again. "New York's a far piece from here. Suppose it'd be mighty hard to check on a marriage done way cross country."

His meal grew cold while he listened to Harv's foolishness. "You want to purchase anything Harv?" Maybe this question would get the man out of Darrell's store and back to his job at the bank.

"Well now, I wanna see your rings. Marie needs to be wearing something to let everyone know she's taken."

As if anyone would want her. Still, Darrell did almost marry her yesterday so that was an unkind and untrue thought.

Reaching under the counter, he pulled out a locked metal box. Opening it, he removed the red pouch and carefully poured the wedding bands onto the counter. Looking at them, he decided to pick one out for himself before putting them away.

Is Willa already wearing a wedding ring?
Funny he hadn't noticed.

He glanced toward the chairs where she sat.
It was empty and her bowl was gone. Had she been
there when Harv suggested that she and Darrell
weren't really married?

When the bell sounded, Darrell greeted the
customer without taking my eyes away from Harv. I
didn't trust the man not to pocket a ring or two, no
matter the family connection between us.

"See anything you like?" He would rather
hurry this man out of the store than make a sale.
The underlying current of animosity coming from
him felt stifling, and Darrell wanted the source of it
gone.

"Sure, but I think I'll bring the little woman
in. Let her pick it out herself." Finally, the man
went out the door and took the trouble he tried to
stir up with him.

Darrell scooped up the merchandise with a
sigh of relief. Locking it away, he greeted the
woman who stood in front of him.

At least Darrell knows about the red-headed man. That thought comforted Willa before another caused her consternation. Since their conversation was interrupted, he didn't know details. Still, she didn't understand the danger well enough to give him specifics.

The bread was made. A piece of salt pork she'd retrieved from the store had been soaked and was even now flavoring a stew of potatoes and carrots. Should she dust or go back downstairs to the store?

Even though customers were in and out, she urgently wanted to speak with Darrell about Harv Perkins. Listening from the stairway, she'd heard the man suggest that their marriage was a ruse. What did Darrell believe?

Perhaps Darrell would know a way to check so they could be sure of their marriage. If only the pastor were in town, it wouldn't matter. They would have married again like Darrell suggested at breakfast.

Did Silver Town have a judge who could marry them? After all, a judge had officiated at the proxy marriage so she knew one had the power to marry couples. It was something to speak about with her husband.

Or was he her husband?

Working in the apartment was comforting to her. She enjoyed the cloistered feel of living and working in the same building. It was like being back at school since she'd rarely left it. The thought that she might not really be Darrell's wife threatened her life and future here.

She started to doubt the people in her life. *Was Aunt Rhoda really her aunt? Did Darrell really send for a proxy bride? Why had a marriage for her seemed the best option to Miss Blackthorn?*

The questions brought to mind another thought. *Do I really have a grandfather who paid for my years at school? Why had he never visited?*

Questions like those could make a woman start questioning her own worth. Thank the Lord her teachers had emphasized self-control.

Also, she sent up thanks that the school's curriculum had included lessons on keeping house as well as cooking. Willa liked to keep busy so she didn't mind her new role as cook and maid. Tomorrow when she had to do laundry might be a different matter, though.

Lifting the lid, she checked the stew and pushed it to the back of the stove, ensuring it wouldn't scorch. Then she returned to the store.

At the bottom of the stairs she stopped, listening for customers. Really, she didn't mind meeting the female shoppers. The men intimidated her, though. Of course, the only men she'd actually met so far, aside from Darrell, were Murphy and Harv Perkins.

Hearing female voices, she left the stairway and entered the store. The number of customers in the store surprised her and made her realize Darrell would need to come up with a way to let her know if he needed help.

The women had organized themselves into three small cliques positioned at different spots in the room. Heads were bent together in all three, whispering.

She noted with some interest that these women were close to her own age. Would some of these women one day be her close friends?

She looked first at the group closest to the door. When the three women there looked back at her, Willa's stomach sank.

Marie and her cronies! *No friends there. What was the woman doing back in the store?*

She ignored that group and went to the young ladies gathered around the sewing supplies. "Can I help you ladies?"

The girls giggled in unison as they turned toward her way. A brown-haired girl asked, "Don't you have to wear an apron to work here? Marie always did."

The blonde next to her leaned in as if to whisper to her friend yet never lowered her voice. "If she didn't care enough to meet the man before she married him, she isn't very discriminating. She probably doesn't care if her clothes get dirty." The girl flashed a determined expression at Willa, ready to do battle.

Both girls looked at her as the conversation amongst the other groups in the room stopped. She felt all of the room staring at her. Looking Darrell's way, she saw worry cloud his usually composed face and shrugged. "Should I assume you don't need any help then?"

When neither responded, she left them to join the two girls warming their hands at the stove. Both gave her a welcoming smile that was like a beacon on a stormy sea to her as she approached.

Ignoring Marie as well as the other young women, Willa chatted with the sisters while the three sat on chairs near the stove. Their names, she learned, were Annabeth and Liza. They'd come to Silver Town last year with their father who worked in a mine called the Silver Queen. Their older brother prospected on the family's claim.

After discovering that they were in the store to sample a few crackers from the barrel that sat by the front door, she invited them upstairs to eat rice and beans left from lunch. Ignoring the dark look her husband sent her way, she refused to allow her new best friends to go hungry.

As she motioned them to proceed her up the stairs, she heard Marie's little girl voice squeak behind her. *She must believe that men find her falsetto attractive.* "You see Darrell! If you'd married me, you'd have someone who actually wanted to help in your store."

Willa didn't wait to hear his response.

CHAPTER 5

As she went upstairs, Darrell wondered why Willa didn't stay to hear his response to Marie's jab. He hoped it meant she didn't care what the woman had to say. It would be best if she could ignore the horrible woman.

He didn't think the Miller sisters were the people he would have chosen as his wife's friends though. Certainly, that attitude showed horrible snobbery, but he felt she should be mixing with the wives of other business owners or women that the pastor's wife might introduce her too.

Turning his gaze from Willa's disappearing back, he looked at Marie. Her eyes narrowed and a malevolent smile contorted her elfin features into an expression that appeared almost demonic. After directing the hellish smile his way, Marie left the shop with her two companions following after her.

Shuddering inwardly at Marie's expression, he directed his attention to the women gathered around the sewing notions. Stepping around barrels, he reached the three women. "What can I interest you ladies in purchasing today?"

Adele Mathers, the brown-haired woman who spoke with such condescension to Willa, tipped her face as if to look down at Darrell, though he towered over her. "Really Mr. Dean, I'm not sure I want to purchase from you. This shop has lost its appeal." The girls next to her nodded and giggled behind their hands.

With determination, he kept his face and voice free of the emotions he felt as he answered her shrewish comment. "Certainly, Mrs. Mathers. I wish you and your husband a good trip when you go to shop in Granger."

Here Darrell had to work hard to keep from snickering. "I'm sure he'll be happy to close his livery and travel on the train for your sewing notions and goods. I believe that is the closest mercantile with items similar to mine."

Taking a rag from his apron pocket, he turned his back on the peevish hens and wiped dust from a shelf. If what they'd experienced today represented the worse of Marie's vengeance, he believed that Willa and he would weather it just fine.

The jingle of the bell drew his attention to the front door. Expecting to see Adele and her cronies leaving the store, it surprised him instead to see Charlie Richards, the station master's son.

"What can I get for you Charlie?" he asked, stuffing the rag into his pocket and moving back behind the counter.

He shifted from one foot to the next before looking Darrell in the eye. "Pa said I was to find out if you were keeping the woman so I can deliver her trunk."

His statement set off whispers amongst the women. *More fodder for the gossips.* Shaking his head at being the subject of Silver Town's rumor mill, Darrell confused Charlie. The young man shrugged his shoulders and made as if to leave.

A little too loudly, Darrell said, "No. Wait." The sharp tone startled both Charlie and the women, who he noticed out the corner of his eye moving closer to the counter.

Clearing his throat, he paused to gain his composure and then continued. "I meant to say that I was, of course, keeping my wife. Please go around to the alley and knock on the door of my rooms. Mrs. Dean is upstairs and will direct you about her trunk." Finished giving Charlie directions, he held out his hand and dropped a dime into Charlie's, not sure if Willa would have money for a tip.

As Charlie left, Albert Crowley passed him in the doorway and entered with a telegram in hand. He placed it on the counter without meeting his gaze. "Sorry, Dean. Found this amongst my papers. Guess I forgot to deliver it after I received the message from your lawyer, Mr. Barrett, last week. I suppose it doesn't matter now, since your bride's here already."

Without waiting for either a response or a tip, Crowley left the store. Picking up the paper, Darrell read the telegram which indicated the date of his bride's arrival. He found it odd Crowley would supposedly find this the day after Willa arrived, when he would no longer be surprised to learn he had a wife on the way.

Is there any actual reason for my sudden prickles of suspicion?

While Crowley wasn't known as a church attending, Christian man, he didn't have a reputation as the town bad guy either. Still, based on his handling of the last telegram, he didn't think he could trust Albert Crowley. Before supper, he decided to put Albert to the test.

Darrell had the sudden desire to travel down to Granger and send a telegram to Mr. Barrett, just to find out if all was above board. *Is Preacher Potter's sister really sick? Did I really send the letter asking for a proxy?* Suddenly answers to those questions seemed almost as necessary as air.

Still, could he really leave the store for a day? Willa was not familiar enough with the people or the business for him to leave her in charge. Then he realized Willa would have to be the one to take the trip.

"What do you mean? I don't want to get on the train again." Did he really say what she thought he did?

"Are you sending me away?" While she was, at least for now, determined to be an obedient wife, this might be where she took a stand.

Darrell shook his head and smiled sweetly at her across the table. They ate the stew and he'd seemed particularly impressed by the fresh bread. He declared they could sell it in the store if Willa could make extra and then casually mentioned putting her back on the train.

"Not on your life! I'm keeping you, wife. Just need you to take the train down to Granger. But you definitely got to come back to me." There was a soft tone that hinted at strong feelings. This surprised her since they'd only known each other a day. Even so, she was sure it was there. Hints of romance peeked through her husband's stoical mask!

Pushing away tender thoughts, she fixed her mind on the issue at hand. "Why doesn't Silver Town have a telegraph office? With the mines, I would expect there to be one."

He smiled ruefully. "Sorry to put you back on that train so quick again. Problem is I can't trust Crowley, the telegraph operator." Then he related about the delayed telegram and shared his suspicions.

A sick feeling gripped Willa's middle. She set down her fork, unable to continue eating. "This is about our marriage, isn't it? Do you think we're married?" No matter how she tried, she couldn't stop the sob that punctuated her last question. She rose from the chair with the idea of fleeing to the bedroom.

He caught her easily before she'd taken more than a few steps. Pulling her backward, he settled her onto his lap. Though she wanted to resist, she gave into her need for comforting and snuggled into his shoulder. Having been held so little in her lifetime, Willa craved his warmth and his comforting touch.

"Now Willa, if there is anything wrong with this proxy marriage the pastor can fix that when he returns from Denver." He tenderly kissed her hair. "Our wedding night was a commitment on my part to this marriage. What about you?"

The solemn tone made his words sound like a vow and reassured her. She nodded against his shoulder and schooled her runaway emotions, as she had been taught, so she could speak without sniffling.

Once again calm, Willa asked about his suspicions. "Please, will you tell me what you suspect and why?"

Darrell's arms squeezed her gently before he spoke with a flat tone, as if he too struggled with his emotions. "When Sarah's father, old Avery died, I inherited part ownership of a local silver mine on condition I marry. I think I told you last night that he and his partner found silver and created this town about four years ago."

When she nodded against his shoulder he continued. "Well, around the time the letter came from the lawyer, Mr. Barrett, Silver Town had a terrible fire and a falling beam injured me."

Her quick intake of breath interrupted him. Even though she could see he was fine, the thought of him being hurt frightened her. Perhaps tender feelings for him already existed in her heart, just as she had earlier suspected he had for her. She was discovering that sexual intimacy was powerful enough to forge such emotions.

He laughed softly and gave her another tender squeeze. "I'm okay now. But I lost a week or so of time."

Pulling away from his shoulder, she looked at him quizzically. "How can you lose time?"

Darrell shrugged and gently pushed her head back to his shoulder. "I like you cuddled against me. Anyhow, I guess my injury caused me not to remember the time. I'm telling you this because my proxy letter dated to that time."

When she stiffened, he moved his hand to her back and began circular motions that soon calmed her. "I know I didn't write the letter since it's not my handwriting. Still, the shaky signature at the bottom sure looks like mine. Tomorrow, I hope to see Mrs. Potter again. She cared for me during that entire time and would know if I asked for a letter to be written."

"Maybe she wrote it." That seemed the obvious answer to her, but Darrell shook his head.

"Looks like it's done by a man's hand. Also Mrs. Potter's handed me enough shopping lists I'd recognize her writing."

Both sat silently for a few minutes. She considered the possibility that he had never actually sent for her.

"Darrell, we both have to travel to Granger. Please we have to find a preacher." She knew her pleading tone hinted at desperation. In truth, she felt trapped. Miss Blackthorn warned her girls to avoid having congress (as she called it) with a man outside of marriage. Without realizing, Willa had done that.

The firm set of Darrell's jaw warned her that he intended to refuse. She held up a hand to stop his answer.

"Consider how this possibility makes me feel. I'm a loose woman after what happened last night." While Willa might feel shame, she still directly met his gaze while watching for his reaction. "I don't blame you, but you are the only one who can fix this for me."

He hung his head a moment and then met her gaze. "You're right, of course. Let's hope the minister in Granger is there and hasn't received a telegram like Revered Potter."

They shared a strained smile over his attempt at humor. She rose from his lap and went to work cleaning the kitchen. With the heavy mood left over from their discussion, she didn't feel that the time was right to speak with Darrell about the red-haired man. Just the thought of the man stirred up a tight fist of terror in her.

She finished her evening chores and Darrell posted a notice in the store's window to indicate it would stay closed for the day. That done they agreed on an early bedtime that night. The train came through the depot early in the morning since Silver Town was the first stop on its run south after leaving Creede.

"Do you want the floor or the bed?" The question shocked Darrell and he whirled toward her in the doorway of the bedroom.

With a suggestive smile on his face, he asked, "Why would I need to sleep on the floor? We're mar…" Understanding flooded his face as he bit off his words.

"If we didn't already plan to marry tomorrow, sleeping on the floor would surely hurry me to that decision," he said with a chuckle.

This affirmed she'd been blessed with a good-humored husband.

CHAPTER 6

Without much success, Darrell tried to keep his bad mood from marring his wife's day. Her gloved hands lay clenched tightly in her lap, and he suspected she struggled with their circumstances.

He reached a hand to her and squeezed her clenched fists within his, trying to reassure her. As he did this, he willed himself to believe all would be well once they found a preacher in Granger and sent out telegrams.

Willa looked up at his touch. He formed what he hoped passed for a reassuring smile instead of a grimace and said, "This too will pass. My father used to say that and it's an expression that has helped me through many a tough time."

She returned the smile. Her hands, resting beneath his, relaxed. The couple sat quietly this way, holding hands for the remainder of the short journey.

Once the train arrived at the Granger depot, Darrell lead Willa to the telegraph office built close by. "I want to send the telegrams first. Maybe we can get a reply before we leave. If not, we'll have to come back to Granger next week."

Offering her his arm, the couple followed the telegraph wires from the depot to the office nearby. They walked along like a courting couple on a Sunday promenade, as if no concerns weighed on them. He smiled down at her and she returned his smile with what he hoped might just be open affection.

Her sea-colored eyes gleamed blue. Already during the few days they'd spent together, he'd noticed they shone green when she felt upset. Blue tinted those eyes when she was calm.

Before going into the office, Darrell squeezed her arm to stop her. "Before we send telegrams, you need to ask if one arrived for Amy Peters," he said with a grave note to my voice.

"Who is Amy Peters? I can't claim someone else's telegram." Her tone and shocked expression affirmed her strong morals. Her stringent ethical code didn't surprise him. He'd already seen how firmly she clung to what she believed was right. After all, he spent last night on the floor rather than cuddled in bed with his wife, in case he didn't happen to be her husband.

To reassure her, he gently patted her hand still resting on his arm. "No need to be concerned, Sweetheart. Amy Peters is a name I made up. I sent a test telegram asking the imaginary Amy to stop her father from leaving town today so that we could marry."

With a sigh he continued, "You know I don't trust Albert Crowley. Let's see if I'm wrong about him being involved in this odd plot I'm sensing."

Inside, they stood in the cramped office and waited at a counter which separated patrons from the operator as well as the telegraph equipment. A young man finished sending a message and jumped up with alacrity.

"How can I help you folks?" He spoke rapidly yet with a courteous tone. Evidently, he simply did most everything in his life fast.

Willa spoke first, inquiring after a telegram for Amy Peters. Her careful wording allowed her to avoid telling a lie.

The telegraph operator shuffled through notes on his desk. Returning to them, he shook his head. "I'm sorry, but it hasn't arrived yet. Where can I find you if'n I do get one?"

Willa looked to Darrell. When she shrugged, she asked the employee to hold on to it and it would be called for by someone. From his smile of relief, he appreciated that answer.

Albert Crowley had failed Darrell again and at the same time proved his suspicions to be real. Acting on those suspicions, he dictated a telegram to Miss Blackthorn as well as one to Mr. Barrett since the man facilitated their proxy marriage, indicating the messenger should wait for a response. He emphasized in each telegram that an immediate reply was needed in Granger and any telegrams sent to Silver Town would not reach him.

Though the telegrams were long and costly, he paid the young man gladly and felt a sense of anticipation. Maybe they would learn something important today to explain the conspiracy they were caught in.

Before leaving the office, Darrell asked the young man about restaurants as well as churches. The telegrapher quickly jabbered about his favorite place to eat as well as the Methodist church he attended. Based on what he said, Darrell let him know where he would be able to find them that day and, offering Willa his arm, left the building.

After the busy streets at home, Granger almost appeared like a ghost town. They made their way through snow-filled streets and past a small mercantile. Its size and the rough condition of the building filled him with pride at his own business. With effort, he tamped that down. If the mine closed due to this panic started by South American silver he'd read about in the newspaper, Silver Town could become as empty as Granger.

At the end of the single street running the length of the town, they found a wooden shack with a crude cross anchored in the ground next to the building's door. Wrapping on the door, Darrell shifted his feet as they waited. What if the preacher had traveled to the mining camps? Many of these missionary preachers rode to the camps during the week, he knew.

While they waited, he joked with Willa. "Good thing he's Methodist or you might not marry me," he said, remembering her asking a few days ago about a Methodist church in Silver Town. It was difficult to believe they'd only met her a few days ago. Darrell felt connected with her in some odd way as if she had been a dear friend for years.

She gave his arm a squeeze and snorted. "Yes, it's your lucky day." Then the look of affection in her eyes drew him in and any words he might have said in response died on his lips. He lost himself in her aqua-eyed gaze and his mouth lowered to meet hers.

The discreet clearing of a throat sounded behind. They jerked apart and guiltily looked at the short, older man who stood in the doorway and waited patiently for one of them to speak.

"Are you the preacher? We're wanting someone to marry us."

He nodded and held out a hand in greeting. "Martin Nelson at your service. Best get the knot done up tight from what I'm seeing." Shaking his head, he opened the door for the erstwhile lovers to enter.

The small church possessed a few rough wooden benches and an altar made out of a board laid on top of two sawhorses. Darrell could care the less about the primitiveness of it. The relief he experienced at the preacher being there so he could marry Willa made even that church seem glorious.

"Please don't think poorly of us," Willa stammered before the pastor could begin the wedding service. Her face had reddened at Preacher Nelson's words. "We thought we were already married but now aren't sure."

His face took on a thoughtful expression. "Surely, there must be an interesting story there, but that's your business."

Typical of a man in the West, he didn't pry. Shaking his head, the pastor left them alone in the church for a few minutes, returning quickly with two men who blinked their eyes as if just waking up.

Then he quickly went to work, turning Darrell's proxy bride into Darrell's lawfully wedded wife. When asked if he had a ring for his bride, he lifted her hand and kissed the band he had placed there the day after she arrived in his life. The all too serious pastor smiled at that.

Satisfaction swamped him when, with a chuckle, the preacher invited Darrell to kiss his bride instead of just her finger. His gaze locked with Willa's as he lowered his face to hers. Delight sparkled in her eyes. Her soft lips melted under his making it an effort to keep the kiss brief.

Producing a certificate from a wooden box hidden in a dark corner of the church, Pastor Nelson indicated where Willa and he would sign. Then he had the witnesses fill in their names. One made his mark instead, so the Pastor wrote the man's name underneath that. Once that was done, Darrell handed each witness a dollar and gave the preacher a five-dollar eagle.

After shaking hands with the happy witnesses and the grateful preacher, Willa and he headed to the small cafe near the depot. With the lunch crowd finishing up, the tables were filled. No one except the newlyweds waited for one to become available.

While they stood, he held her hand and teased, "Bet you never dreamed your wedding would be like that."

She giggled and sighed happily. "I always hoped I'd have a groom who gazed at me with admiration and affection so you're wrong. I just had my dream wedding."

Darrell decided then God above had looked out for him when Willa arrived in Silver Town. Sharing that thought with her sent a jolt of embarrassment through him, making him squirm inwardly. Instead of allowing her to sense the unease he had about what he'd said, Darrell quickly shifted to a new topic. "It's like the verse in Romans. I think it's in the eighth chapter where

Paul wrote about all things working out good for the people who love God."

She nodded, "I see what you mean. Someone is creating mischief, yet it brought us together. What a lovely way to think about it." Then she resumed with a thoughtful look, "It's Romans 8:28, by the way."

He squeezed her hand, wishing they weren't in public so he could kiss her instead. For the last five years, he had easily restrained from physical intimacy with anyone. His new wife's presence caused a dam to break inside, he realized, so now he craved to touch her and be with her.

Seeing a table become empty, the suddenly worried man led her to it and pulled out a chair for her. How would he deal with the emotions that rushed through him? God willing, he wouldn't lose his stoical demeanor with anyone else.

Sitting, they waited for someone to clean the table as well as bring menus. A harried looking woman with tendrils of wilted brown hair escaping a lopsided bun rushed to remove the dirty dishes but didn't bother to wipe the surface. Without offering a menu, she scampered to the kitchen and returned with two plates of beef stew.

At their surprised look, she gave a tight-lipped smile. "Gus makes one thing each day, in case you're wondering." She set the stew in front of the couple. "I'll be back with cups and the coffee pot."

Convinced that more than ever he needed to pray over the meal, Darrell bowed his head and asked that the food would bless their bodies and not harm them. Then he reached for his spoon and took a tentative taste.

Gus, whoever he was, certainly knew how to cook!

The waitress returned with coffee. After that, and just as they were finishing the stew, she produced a plate of bread. Across from him, his wife hid her giggles behind her hand. If there had been a napkin, she might have used that to hide her giggles. Then he had the silly thought that maybe the waitress would bring napkins next.

Finished with the meal, Darrell worriedly checked the time. They had only a little over an hour before the train came through on its northern route. Still, he thought they should head to the depot since trains notoriously deviated from posted time schedules.

Keeping an ear to the wind for any sound of the train, he guided Willa through the snow and back to the telegraph office. Dots and dashes filled the air and the operator they'd met earlier hurriedly wrote on a pad. With any luck, that message would be for them.

At last the telegraph went silent. Asking them to wait a minute, he watched as the operator rewrote his message on paper with Western Union's masthead at the top. When done, he handed over the paper.

"Well, we came back at a good time," Darrell laughingly told him.

Where has my stoicism gone? This change he continued to experience since Willa's arrival confused him. He hardly recognized either himself or the bubble of joy he carried around in his chest since the good Lord dropped Willa into his life.

The young man only nodded and reached behind him to the desk. He pulled another telegram from a pile. "Sorry I couldn't get away from the telegraph to deliver this one."

Reassuring him it didn't matter he handed the telegrapher a quarter as a tip. Since the day was cold, he urged Willa, "Have a seat on the bench by the door while I read the messages."

In the first, Miss Blackthorn expressed her alarm at the possibility of Willa's marriage being false and urged Darrell to find a preacher to rectify that. In addition, she promised to hire the Pinkerton detectives to investigate both in New York as well as in Silver Town. They should expect a detective to arrive as quickly as train schedules allowed.

The second telegram came from Mr. Young rather than his partner. He expressed regret that Barrett was out of the office but emphasized no action should be taken. He wrote Darrell especially should, under no circumstances, marry Willa a second time. As he read that, the hackles on the back of Darrell's neck rose. Why should this lawyer care if they arranged to have a preacher marry them? How could it be a mistake for him and Willa to marry?

At the telegrapher's announcement of "Train's coming," they hurried out the door and across the short distance to the depot. Darrell looked behind him for Willa and saw she lagged behind and bent over as if picking something up off the ground.

Curious and concerned, he retraced his steps to her side. "Are you all right Wi--?"

She hit his leg, cutting him off before he said her name completely! Then he noticed a scarred, red-haired man staring from across the street. At the sound of the train's whistle and the conductor's call of "All aboard," he grabbed Willa's arm and hurried her onto the train.

As they ascended the few steps into the train car a voice behind them called, "Wait one minute, Willa VanDurring. I'm going to..."

The train chugged out of the depot even before they seated themselves. Darrell couldn't tell if they ran to catch the train or to escape from the man Miss Blackthorn cautioned Willa to avoid.

CHAPTER 7

The red-haired man was real! After catching not even a glimpse of him on her trip west, Willa began to wonder if he really posed a threat. With Darrell's help, she narrowly escaped someone who she thought of as a figment of Roger the groundskeeper's imagination!

Wondering what he wanted with her kept Willa deep in thought as the train returned them to Silver Town. For whatever reason, Darrell didn't speak either. She wanted to cry as she thought of how isolated the gulf between them made her feel, separated while physically next to each other. What a disappointing end their wedding trip!

Once in Silver Town, Darrell helped her down the steps of the railway carriage and lifted her trembling hand into the crook of his arm. He smiled and Willa felt the warmth of it penetrate her worry while erasing any distance between them that she'd imagined earlier. Sighing with relief, she gave him a half smile in return.

As they approached home and the mercantile, Willa noticed Mrs. Potter walking away from the closed shop. Waving to get her attention, she urged Darrell to hurry.

"Hello, Mrs. Potter. Have you had any news about your husband's sister?" Willa asked with sincere interest. After all, it seemed suspicious for the preacher to be called out of town just when Darrell and she hoped he would marry them.

Mrs. Potter wore a look of surprise at seeing the couple, probably because the sign on the door indicated they'd be out of town. After a brief pause, the look of surprise changed to one of confusion. "My sister-in-law isn't even in Denver."

Her confused expression morphed into irritation. "Reverend Potter traveled all that way. When he went to the hotel, no one there had even heard of her. After sending a wire, he learned she is healthy and at home in Pennsylvania." Mrs. Potter gave an indelicate snort to punctuate her last sentence, as if her sister-in-law had done something wrong by being in good health.

Stifling a giggle at her snort, Willa changed topics. "Did you need something from the store? My husband would be glad to help you, I'm sure."

Mrs. Potter smiled and put a motherly hand on my arm, "No my dear, I merely wanted to assure you both the reverend would be back in town in another two days. He'll be happy to marry you then."

Darrell cut into the conversation. With a satisfied grin, he said, "No need now Mrs. Potter. We traveled to Granger and had the Reverend Nelson tie up the knot. Didn't want any whispers in the community about whether we were really married since it was done by proxy."

Mrs. Potter congratulated them warmly on their marriage. Just before leaving her Darrell asked, "By the by, did you happen to write a letter for me last year, right after the fire, requesting a bride by proxy?"

Her blank expression answered his question. Her tone, though, was frosty. "No, I certainly nursed you through that time, but I would never have written a letter like that without your permission."

Quickly apologizing, Darrell explained about the mysterious letter. Mollified, she commented, "Odd things seemed to be happening lately, with your letter as well as the telegram sent to lure my husband away from town."

After exchanging a few more niceties, they parted with the newlyweds entering the alleyway before climbing the stairs to our rooms. After unlocking the door, Darrell swung his bride into his arms and carried her from the landing into the apartment.

Laughing, she hugged an arm around his neck and pulled his face down to kiss his cheek. Just as she almost touched her lips to his skin, he turned his face and gave her a heated kiss.

After lifting his lips, he chuckled. "That floor was mighty uncomfortable last night Willa. I sure am looking forward to going to bed tonight."

The suggestion in his words brought a blossom of deep pink to her cheeks and caused him to grin broadly.

Trying to distract him from that topic she suggested, "I think we should make a list of everything we believe to be suspicious."

Darrell nodded his head, "I didn't show you the telegrams, but your former guardian seems concerned and is sending a Pinkerton out to investigate." He pulled the two telegrams from his pocket and handed them to her.

Putting an arm around her and hugging her shoulders tenderly, he continued. "I like your idea about a list. We'll give it to the detective after he arrives."

While Willa scrambled eggs and made pancakes for a quick supper, Darrell sat the table and silently wrote. Every once in a while, he stopped to stare off into the distance as if that helped him remember details.

Though she didn't say anything, she felt left out. He'd been such a perfect groom that day she expected him to be the ideal husband as well. Willa felt let down, believing that they would make the list together so that she had input into what they gave the Pinkerton. For some reason, it seemed to her Darrell thought what she might have to say was of no importance.

So, she cooked and mentally stewed. When Darrell broke the silence, his words had her dropping her head with shame. "There, I've put down what I know. Would you read it over and add your thoughts? Change anything I've written that's not accurate."

With those few words, she learned something new about him. He valued her opinion and wanted to know her ideas. She should have asked him rather than making assumptions and pouting about them.

After the meal, Willa cleaned the kitchen and sat down to read his list. He'd detailed his suspicions about the proxy letter and the telegram sent to the preacher. She added about Perkins's hurried marriage to Marie as well as the few details she knew about the red-haired man. Though the mysterious man was probably not connected to the doubtful events around their proxy marriage, something in her mind urged her to include it.

Finished, she forgot about the list for the night and took Darrell's hand. Not every girl had the good fortune to enjoy two wedding nights with the same groom.

During the next week, Darrell and she evolved rather easily from groom and bride to husband and wife. They settled into a routine, and Willa was surprised by how comfortable she felt. Perhaps it was because he was a creature of habit.

Having no memories of residing anywhere but the Academy, living by a strict routine was all she knew. Because of that, Darrell's daily schedule helped her to adjust.

As the next days passed, many friendly townspeople introduced themselves, showing they were unaffected by Marie's dislike of her. She also deepened her friendship with Annabeth and Liza Miller. During one of their visits, Willa learned an interesting piece of news about the mine Darrell had lost to Harv Perkins.

That morning when they visited, she noticed how sad both appeared. Even their shoulders sagged. Immediately, Willa asked what had happened.

Liza shook her head sadly. "The Silver Queen closed. Dad's out of a job. With no warning at all!" Indignation dripped from her last comment.

The suddenness of the closure caught her attention. She asked, "Did you hear why it closed?"

Annabeth shook her head, "Nothin' except Harv Perkins inherited half. Must be Mr. Walters don't wanna share since he scampered out of town with the profits. Thank goodness for us he waited 'til after the miners' payday to leave."

Willa now knew why neither Perkins nor his wife visited the store last week. Darrell mentioned his surprise when Harv didn't come to gloat about the inheritance. She'd expected more screaming attacks by Marie and agreed that she found it odd when neither approached them.

Bringing her attention back to the conversation, Willa made a noise she hoped sounded sympathetic. "Has Harv Perkins told the miners he would get the Silver Queen started up again?"

Annabeth's voice held a remorse tone as she answered. "Nah. Dad said it had something to do with the President and Sherman Silver. Have you heard of any of those things?"

Because Miss Blackthorn insisted, Willa read the papers daily so she did know about the silver panic as well as Sherman Silver and tried to explain them to the sisters. President Cleveland convinced Congress to repeal the Sherman Silver Purchase Act. Willa didn't realize this would halt mining, though. Perhaps Darrell would know what was happening with the Silver Queen and why.

By the end of the visit, she had several loaves of bread baked. Sending two loaves with the sisters, she encouraged them to visit again. Their chats helped keep her from missing friends she'd left at school.

The week also brought a development in the threat from the red-haired man. Darrell spoke with the stationmaster about him, giving a description and asking Mr. Richards to send Charlie to the store right away if a man answering such a description arrived by train.

Two days later, Charlie Richards delivered goods brought by train that morning. Upstairs, she heard Darrell's angry shout. Alarmed, she rushed down the stairs and had to grab the railing when her foot slipped on one of the narrow treads. Once she righted herself, Willa continued with more care and safely reached the doorway into the store.

Peeking around the door jamb, she watched Darrell grab up the shotgun kept below the counter. He placed it within easy reach on the counter as he glared at Charlie.

"What in the name of my sainted Miss Blackthorn is going on in here?" Willa protested with hands on hips. Then she surveyed the store. The few customers looked back at her in confusion.

Darrell frowned and pointed at Charlie. "Go ahead and tell her." Picking up the gun, he cracked it open to be sure a shell was in place.

Charlie gulped nervously. "I'm just doing as Mr. Dean said. Bringing news. A man got off the train today that was like he warned Dad and me about. Has red hair and this really wicked scar on the side of his face."

She only nodded, controlling her emotions. "Thank you, Charlie. I am glad you told us. Did you happen to speak with the man?"

Charlie shook his head. "Dad did. He asked him for directions to a hotel. Dad sent him to the Rio Grande, of course." He added, "We always do, it being new and the nicest one."

Thanking Charlie, Willa then cajoled her husband. "The man hasn't actually harmed me. All we have to go by are Miss Blackthorn's fears and drunken threats heard by an equally drunk man."

Darrell nodded, "Suppose so, but it's my job to see you safe." He looked at three women hiding in a shadowy corner of the store. "Ladies, I do apologize for any fright. May I help you with anything?"

The women responded in chorus, "Not right now Mr. Dean." Their voices were high, as if from fright or excitement. Willa noticed Adele Mathers in the group.

Catching that woman's eye, Willa smugly donned the extra white apron Darrell kept in the store. She had made such a fuss about her not wearing it the last time they'd met. The woman frowned and whispered to the other two, their heads huddled together.

Taking over the store for Darrell, Willa assured him all would be fine. "After all, my would-be pursuer had just arrived in town and shouldn't pose a threat yet," she reasoned.

With a torn expression, Darrell looked between Charlie and her before nodding. Taking the shotgun with him, Darrell and Charlie left through the door to the storeroom. In the alley, a door led directly into that room, she knew. As he went, Darrell told her he would be in and out of the store by way of that door.

With rag in hand, she knelt on the floor and wiped dust from the lowest shelves to the left of the front door. She planned to start there and work her way around the room. Darrell swept each morning and still those shelves became dirty more quickly than the others. Perhaps the daily sweeping stirred up the dirt and caused their filthy state.

Humming, she worked steadily and had reached the corner. Beginning the first shelf along the next wall, she called, "Be right with you," when the bell above the front door sounded.

A man's voice responded, "Get over here now!"

Her spine stiffened at his rudeness. Prickles of fear ran through her for some unknown reason. She rose from her knees to face a red-haired man.

"We didn't expect you yet," she calmly said, even though she felt like a cornered rabbit. Inside Willa prayed for safety and for her husband to come.

The man looked confused and rubbed his scarred cheek. "Were expecting me, huh? Suppose you learned I was coming for you. He wanted to meet you before I finished you. Not anymore though."

Maybe some courage came from her gun-toting husband who worked not far away or perhaps she'd simply grown tired of living in fear. Instead of feigning calm, she roared hoping Darrell would hear, "Just who are you and why are you threatening me?"

The customers, already shocked by the appearance of Darrell's shotgun and the menacing man, stood with mouths agape at the shout. Except for Adele, who stared at her with a satisfied smile.

Apparently, she expected a proxy bride to behave like a harridan, based on her malicious grin. Surprisingly the women didn't leave the store.

Then Willa realized they couldn't. The man blocked the front door where he stood.

Badly dressed and rumpled from his train trip, Willa decided the man must be a thug like the Five Points Gang or the Bowery Boys she read about in the paper. His accent proclaimed him from

New York. Strange information to think about! It didn't help her at all to understand who sent him.

She tried again, this time adding a whimper to her voice. She hoped he'd think she was afraid--which she was--and begin boasting about the job he'd been sent to do. "Well, aren't you going to tell me why you want to hurt me?"

He responded by grinning cruelly and removing a thin chain from the pocket of his tattered dark wool overcoat coat. Twisting it around both of his hands, he formed a sort of garrote with it.

"By the time I got myself to Blackthorn's Academy, you were gone," he growled. "Your trail went cold until my client heard his secretary remark about your proxy marriage in Mr. Barrett's office. I got a lucky break being that those secretaries eat lunch together."

Whimpering accomplished nothing so she yelled again. "My guardian said you threatened me with harm. It's why I married by proxy."

Her adversary chuckled. "Someone hid your trail pretty good. Took me awhile. I expect I know who tried to stop me too."

His chuckle sent hot rage through her. She put her hands on her hips and glared. "Well, you can get on the train and leave Silver Town or I'll find a way to make your life miserable. I am not going to be bullied."

Separating herself from the situation, it seemed to Willa like she watched a play similar to those older students attended with Miss Blackthorn in the city. The man planned to choke her with a chain and as a defense she'd ordered him back on the train? A giggle escaped her at that absurdity or perhaps because of her nervous fear.

The red-haired man's mouth also hung open in shock when he heard that giggle. Good! She had the advantage and decided to use it.

Rushing, she moved toward the storeroom. Seeing where she headed, he quickly jumped in the same direction to cut her off. He now stood directly in front of the door to the room that promised help.

"Now why you want to go off and leave me before I tell you who wants you dead." A gasp from one of the women reminded her others watched. No wonder she'd compared this to a play. They even had an audience.

At the noise, both of them looked at the women. Perhaps he just then realized they were there. He suddenly put the chain back in his pocket. Before anything more happened, the store room door swung open and the villain fell to his knees.

Darrell flew in, his shotgun ready. The thug vaulted to his feet and gained the front door. He left before Darrell could even take aim.

With a shotgun he didn't really need to aim. That confused her and she asked him about it. "Why didn't you shoot him as you came through the door?"

Moving to the counter, Darrell put down the gun and possessively embraced his wife. "I didn't want any of the scattered shot to hit you, Sweetheart." He sounded out of breath as he answered and squeezed her tightly.

Keeping his arms around her, Darrell focused on the women huddled in that same shadowy corner. "Are any of you ladies hurt? Should I fetch your husbands for you?"

Each shook her head and, as a group, they edged to the door and left. Probably to tell the story around town, Willa speculated. After all, it wasn't every day the apparently emotionless Darrell Dean lost his cool and brandished a shotgun or that a villain tried to kill a woman with a chain.

CHAPTER 8

Silver Town buzzed with gossip about the man who tried to kill the mercantile owner's wife. Their town didn't have an actual sheriff, relying on the men who ran security at the mine. Darrell knew they needed that Pinkerton to hurry up and get here.

Other business owners armed themselves and joined him to hunt for the New York assassin. Even Big Murphy and his bouncer surprised Darrell by grabbing shotguns and taking part in the search. They raced throughout the town checking boarding houses, the hotel and saloons.

As Charlie Richards' wagon was only partially unloaded, he removed one horse from the harness and rode it bareback up the side of the mountain. He'd be sure his father was up to date on the news. Darrell needed the man to be on the lookout for the criminal as well as to start carrying a side arm himself.

Though he hated leaving her alone, he told Willa to stay in the apartment and locked both the door to the rooms and the front door of the mercantile. Since he kept the backdoor to their rooms locked, he didn't bother with it.

If the murderer watched from some hidden spot, Darrell wanted the man they hunted to believe Willa was now alone in the store. To that end, he asked Mathers to hide nearby and watch the backdoor of their rooms and the door into the storeroom. Harv Perkins offered to keep an eye on the front of the store. Though Darrell didn't like the idea, he doubted the red-haired man would try to enter that way as it was too public. He shrugged and thanked the man for his offer.

Heading to the hotel, the spot between his shoulders burned. Was it his imagination or did someone have a gun centered on him?

Relieved, he reached the hotel. Bert, the day clerk, stood with a rifle pointed at the front door as he entered.

"Lower that rifle and tell me if a red head with a scarred left cheek's been here today." He spoke with a commanding tone, hoping it intimidated the clerk. The man and Albert Crowley were drinking buddies, he'd heard, so Darrell didn't trust him.

Bert's rifle never deviated from the door. He answered with a clipped, impatient tone. "Haven't seen him and hope I don't. Don't want trouble here."

Hours later, when the searchers met up outside the store, no one had any news. The thug simply disappeared. He ground his teeth in frustration.

Thinking about it, he imagined the man could easily hide out at the Silver Queen mine. Only a few men guarded it to keep thieves away, he'd heard. A desperate man could slip past them. Still, in winter, it would be a cold place to hide and the newly arrived criminal wouldn't know about it so he dismissed that idea.

Someone in town must be hiding him. It's the only way he could disappear so quickly.

Immediately Murphy came to mind. He surprised him by his willingness to help search. Maybe he wanted to divert suspicions away from himself when he realized that the thug had to be hiding in town.

One more thing for Willa to add to their list.

What delayed that Pinkerton?

Early the next morning, persistent knocking woke Darrell. Grabbing first his pants and then the loaded shotgun, he hurried to the door. Before opening it, he barked, "Who's there?"

A low and rough male voice said, "Pinkerton," but nothing else.

Not yet sure he could trust him, Darrell challenged him with the only question he could think of that early in the morning. "Who hired you?"

The voice responded, "A woman named Blackthorn."

Wanting to let Willa know about the man, he hissed, "Wait out there just a bit longer. I'll be back quick." Rushing into the bedroom, he explained to an already awake Willa about their visitor and both dressed quickly.

By the time Dennis Leary sat at their table, Willa had coffee brewing in her new pot and stood by the table holding her suspicions list. The small, nondescript man silently took it from her and read it. When he raised his head, he showed no surprise or concern. Disappointment at his lack of response danced across Willa's face.

She could not resist prodding the man. "What do you think? Is Harv Perkins at fault?"

Leary had sat deep in thought after reading our list. At her question, he finally spoke. "I don't work that fast ma'am. First, I want to nose around town."

The Pinkerton switched his focus from Willa to him. "Before I go snooping around, I want to ask you a few questions."

Nodding his head, Darrell gave him permission. However, the detective stayed silent for a moment. "Did you know your wife before she arrived here?"

Was he suspicious of Willa? "No, she came here as both a stranger and a surprise. Can't say I'm disappointed that she's here," reaching out, he gripped Willa's hand and brought it to his lips for a kiss.

The detective made a gargled sound of embarrassment before continuing. "Mrs. Dean, did the man who attacked you say anything that could hint at who sent him?"

At her grimace Darrell knew she hated reliving that moment. Nonetheless, she rolled her eyes upward to help herself think through it again. "He claimed his employer wanted to meet me before the red-haired man killed me. Then he said that had changed."

Wanting to comfort her, her husband rose and wrapped an arm around her shoulders. She looked at him and smiled weakly.

Within his arms, Darrell felt her stiffen before she spoke. "Wait! He did say something that might be important. The person who hired him has a secretary who lunches with Mr. Barrett's secretary." That was new information to him. He hadn't pushed her last night to talk about her attack. He feared speaking about it before bedtime might cause her nightmares. Even with that precaution she'd had terrible dreams.

She smiled triumphantly when she remembered this bit of information before her face quickly clouded over. "If the man knew about our proxy marriage why did he call me Miss VanDurring when he saw us in Granger? Did he know the proxy marriage was false?"

Leary gave her a measuring stare and then nodded. "I'll send a few telegrams tomorrow. See what I can discover about Barrett's office and his secretary."

Shaking his head and with a tone of disgust he couldn't hide, Darrell said, "Albert's not a very honest telegraph operator."

Dennis Leary's mouth lifted into a wide grin. He looked like a kid about to receive a present. With great confidence he said, "I'm sure I can persuade the man to behave from here on out."

Husband and wife exchanged a look of satisfaction. With this man on the job, they would get to the heart of the problem and discover the identity of their enemy. Before he left, Leary asked a few more questions and they filled him in on the situation as best as they could.

When Darrell held the backdoor open for him to leave, he shared one more possible lead. "Leary, you might want to interview the three female customers who witnessed the act." When he agreed, Darrell told him who they were and where to find each. Shutting and locking the door behind him, he mentally wished him luck. They all could use some.

Dawn tinted the sky a soft pink, letting him know it was still early morning. Moving the short distance from the door to where Willa stood, Darrell took her hand and asked, "What do you think about Dennis Leary?"

Her face held a thoughtful look and she said nothing. Then she shook her head and sighed. "I trust him to do the best job he can for us. We'll see just how good he is in the next few days, I expect."

Wanting to distract her from the worry he heard in her voice, he lowered his mouth to the back of her neck and kissed the ticklish spot he'd found there that first night they'd been together. "Come back to bed with me Sweetheart. I want to remind you we're still newlyweds."

That did the trick. She giggled and pulled her hand from his to race into their bedroom. Once there, she started slowly unbuttoning her shirtwaist. They both forgot about any concerns and enjoyed being married.

CHAPTER 9

"You're married?" The disappointed woman glared after Willa introduced Darrell as her husband.

Charlie Richards stood at the door, wringing his hands. The angry tone must have upset him. Maybe he felt guilty about bringing the nasty woman to his store.

Clearing his throat to get Charlie's attention he asked, "Did she arrive with luggage?" At his nod Darrell turned back to Willa's aunt. "Miss VanDurring, we don't have room for a guest. Shall I have Charlie take your luggage to the hotel?"

Though a short woman, she managed to look down her nose at him as she responded. "No guestroom? Well, I suppose needs must. Yes, I will stay at the hotel while I decide if you are misusing my niece."

Giving a sigh of relief at escaping the woman's presence, Charlie moved to the door. Even a call to wait for a tip didn't halt him. Knowing how he felt, Darrell stood there wishing he could leave too.

Determined to protect his wife, he focused on the aunt's jabbering. "—and I told you I would give you a home. This marriage is an extreme measure. I can't think that your guardian had your best interests at heart."

Willa put up a hand to stop her aunt. "Whatever else you might say, I won't tolerate any criticisms of either Miss Blackthorn or my husband. We don't know each other Aunt Rhoda so I will tell you I tenaciously protect those I love."

She just admitted to loving him. Elation filled him with bubbles of joy. Darrell wanted to shout with happiness. However, he worked to keep his expression blank as he waited for Rhoda's response.

The look that filled her eyes might have been hatred, but she masked it quickly. Instead she plastered a look of resignation on her face and spoke with a hurt tone as she held her hands out imploringly. "I only want to fulfill your dear mama's dying wish that I look out for you."

With artfully arranged blonde sausage curls cascading over her shoulder and the delicate froth of her ruffled pink gown, Rhoda VanDurring appeared innocent, angelic almost. So why did the woman raise the hackles on the back of his neck?

With a look in Darrell's direction, Willa asked, "Do you mind if I take Aunt Rhoda upstairs for a cup of tea? I hate to leave you out of our conversation, but I am sure she needs refreshment after her long trip." Rhoda's expression changed to one of triumph when Willa spoke of the two of them going off alone. This further raised his suspicions about her purpose in coming to Silver Town.

However, he didn't worry about what the woman would say to Willa when they were alone. She had skill in handling difficult people and wouldn't allow Rhoda to manipulate her, he was sure.

Giving her a quick kiss on her cheek, he assured her, "I'll survive without being part of the conversation." Then he turned away to help the customer who had entered the store.

Actually, very little time passed before they returned from upstairs. "Aunt Rhoda is fatigued so I'll walk her to the hotel," Willa told her husband, before she and her aunt left the store. Her aunt tossed him a smug, clearly satisfied look. About what, he couldn't be sure. He did notice that Willa had a tense look around her mouth that worried him a bit.

The fact Willa didn't immediately return escaped his notice, as busy as the store was that day. The sudden appearance of a very frightened Mrs. Potter had him remembering Willa was still gone.

Bringing an air of terror with her, the pastor's wife hurried into the store. Stopping in front of the counter, she wrung her hands and wailed, "Mrs. Dean collapsed in the street! You must go quickly to the Widow Fremont's house.

Don't worry about the store. I'll watch it." With a quick hand, she grabbed at his arm and added, "She said to bring her alum and black tea."

Moving to the glass jars behind the counter, Darrell filled small paper bags with both items as rapidly as his shaking hands allowed. That done, he raced out the door without even a grabbing a coat. The town desperately needed a doctor. Though the widow had skill in setting bones or stitching wounds, this sounded mysterious. Would she have the knowledge to diagnosis and treat his wife?

As he ran, Darrell dodged surprised townspeople. A few shouted, "Where's the fire?" If he responded at all, he shouted, "Willa's sick." On the run, he nevertheless noted Aunt Rhoda. She had just left the telegraph office and, as he raced past her, she smiled that same smug grin she'd worn at the store a while earlier.

As he ran pass the bank, he met Leary leaving it. The man noticed him and started running along with him. "What's happened?" he asked as they both hurried.

At this point because of fear and the exercise, Darrell barely had enough breath to speak. "Willa...collapsed," he managed to get out.

The widow lived behind the bank so they reached her house not long after Leary joined him. Without knocking, both entered. Immediately, Darrell started calling the widow's name. When she responded, the men followed her voice to a small bedroom off from her kitchen.

Seeing Darrell enter, her brow wrinkled with worry and words tumbled from her, "It must be ptomaine poisoning Mr. Dean or maybe milk sickness. But it's winter. I wouldn't expect that."

He shook his head vehemently. "No, we ate the same things today. This came on suddenly, just after she visited with her aunt."

After saying that, he looked over his shoulder to Leary who stood behind him. "Can you manage to see the telegram Rhoda VanDurring sent a few minutes ago?"

Leary nodded, concern apparent on his typically reserved face, and left without saying anything. Darrell focused his attention on the widow and held out the paper bags. With worry etched deeply into the groves of her face, she took them and moved into her kitchen.

Sitting on the edge of the bed where Willa lay curled and groaning, her husband rubbed her back. When he touched her, she flinched away and moaned with pain. Since he couldn't touch her, he spoke soothingly to her.

"Dearest one, I need to you to get better. I can't imagine life without you, even after only a few weeks together." It didn't stop her moaning. However, some of the stiffness in her body seemed to melt when she heard his voice.

"Please, my love, tell me if you ate anything while with your aunt." As he spoke, he sat on his hands to keep from touching her. The need to stroke her hair or rub her back burned strongly in him. On their first full day together, he promised to protect her. Yet here she lay, possibly dying.

"Tea…" She wheezed out that one word before adding another, "Bitter." After saying that much, she resumed groaning and curled herself tightly around her gut.

He needed to know one more thing. "Did your aunt supply the tea leaves?"

Watching her closely, he caught her quick nod. That nod confirmed his suspicions. Her aunt came to Silver Town to harm Willa. No wonder he experienced prickles of alarm when he looked at the woman.

Mrs. Fremont returned to the bedroom with a bucket and a tin cup. "Since she didn't complain about her throat being on fire, I think it's safe to bring up whatever's down in her." She looked at Darrell intensely, willing him to understand what they had to do.

Between her stern voice and intense look as well as Willa's desperate health, any hesitance he might have had disappeared. "Once she drinks this alum mixture, this isn't going to be pleasant. Just remember that 'in sickness and in health' vow you made Mr. Dean. I need your help and can't have you going wiggly on me here." He nodded briskly to signal she should go ahead.

Telling him to put an arm behind his wife, the widow had him raise her up to drink from the tin cup. Willa's reaction came quickly, partially filling the bucket with the contents of her stomach. They repeated the process until she couldn't bring up anything more. Without tight self-control he might have added to the bucket, as nauseous as he now felt.

Once Willa finished vomiting, Mrs. Fremont left the room and he allowed her to lie back onto the bed. She moaned weakly but stretched out and no longer writhed. The widow's treatment had helped.

The woman carried another tin cup into the room. "More alum?" he asked, dreading going through all of that again.

She shook her graying head. "Not this time. Strong black tea to soothe her stomach cramps. As soon as she drinks this, we'll see if more treatment might be called for."

Nodding at Willa, Mrs. Fremont indicated he should lift her again. He crooned into her ear, coaxing her to sip the tepid tea the widow had made, at the same time as the alum mixture she told him.

By the time she managed several sips, his wife appeared to be exhausted but at peace. The pain that gripped her had left. The widow declared her on the mend, "Though it was a close thing, to be sure. She must have gotten only a small dose of the poison or I doubt I could have saved her."

Thanking the woman, he asked, "When can I take her home? She's in danger, and I can't keep her secure here." He said this with an apologetic look since he didn't want the woman to believe he thought she wouldn't protect Willa. Still, she'd be safer isolated in their rooms.

Looking into the widow's face, Darrell almost audibly sighed with relief to see she hadn't taken offense. Thinking aloud she said, "I'd best watch her for several more hours. Might be able to get a man in here to guard the door."

Accepting her decision, he left Willa with her and went to find Leary. He checked at the telegraph office first. Crowley hung his head, refusing to look at Darrell, and mumbled that Leary had left about an hour ago.

Next, he made his way to the Rio Grande Hotel. In the lobby, Leary leaned over the front desk and shook Bert by the collar. At his approach the Pinkerton spun rapidly and then relaxed when he recognized him. "Hope your being here means your woman's on the mend," he growled out in his low, gravelly voice before again facing Bert.

The desk clerk inched his way toward the open office door. Leary barked out, "Hold on there," which sent the unsavory man scurrying quickly toward it. When he reached it, he slammed the door and an audible click signaled he'd locked it.

Filling Leary in on Willa's condition, Darrell asked him if he had any idea what was in Rhoda's telegram. He might be jumping to an erroneous conclusion. Still, Darrell couldn't shake the conviction that Willa's aunt tried to kill her.

The Pinkerton's hand gestured toward two chairs, and they sat down. "Interesting telegram," he growled. "It read 'W. drank' and nothing else. You know what that might mean."

Pounding a fist angrily into his hand, Darrell repeated what his wife said about the tea Rhoda VanDurring had her try. The detective's lips compressed and his eyes narrowed. "Sounds like that woman has something to answer for in all of this."

Leary met his gaze and continued. "Got an interesting telegram from that lawyer, Mr. Barrett. Seems your wife's grandfather is at death's door. A large sum of money will come your wife's way if she's alive at the time of his death. If she's already dead, then her aunt inherits the entire fortune."

The detective stopped to roll and light a cigarette.

He waited patiently, not wanting to interrupt Leary's thoughts. Finally, the man shared his deductions with Darrell. "Seems to me two separate things are happening here. One's this fake marriage to cheat you out of an inheritance. The other is the danger your wife's in. Two different things, but both involve inheritances."

Watching the smoke ring he blew disappear, he spoke with a note of authority in his voice. "I can't worry too much about your inheritance or who sent that fake proxy. We need to be looking for that man who attacked your wife so we can figure out if anyone beside her aunt wants her dead."

With elbows resting on the arms of the chair, Darrell exhaustedly laid his head in his hands and groaned. "I don't care about the Silver Queen mine or who cheated me out of it. I just want to get whoever is after my wife."

Then a thought came to mind that straightened him up in his chair. "There isn't any law in Silver Town. Will Rhoda VanDurring get away with what she's done?"

Leary shrugged. "Not sure yet. I sent a telegram asking for the Colorado Rangers to come. Hopefully the Pinkerton name will bring them on the run. So far, I have the woman locked in her room. I was just convincing Bert to leave her in there when you walked into the hotel."

Something he had wondered about suddenly seemed extremely important. "Leary, do you suppose Barrett can get the grandfather to tell him why he hid Willa away from her aunt fifteen years ago? It might be a key to understanding this mystery."

The detective stubbed out his cigarette in a nearby ashtray and rose. "I've got that Crowley over at the telegraph office behaving now. Think I'll go send Barrett a wire. Maybe he knows something already." With a purposeful stride, he left the hotel.

Before he followed him out, Darrell knocked on the office door. "Bert, he's gone."

The door opened a crack and then a little wider. Bert left the office and took a wide path around him to head toward the stairs leading to the rooms. he stopped him, moving to put himself in the desk clerk's path. "She's guilty, Bert. The woman admitted it in a telegram, and Willa's few words confirmed what happened."

Here his famous control slipped a little. Something almost resembling a sob escaped Darrell, and he stopped speaking for a moment. Once composed he continued, "I can't keep my wife safe if the woman who wants to kill her runs loose around town."

The man looked at him solemnly for a moment and then nodded. Giving his vest a nervous tug to straighten it, he agreed to leave Rhoda locked in her room.

"Thanks Bert. The Colorado Rangers are on their way to Silver Town to take care of her," he assured him. "Sorry ahead of time if she yells or disrupts things. Just know putting up with trouble from her is saving a life, and I'm in your debt."

Bert's face first showed a speculative gleam and then satisfaction at the thought of Darrell owing him a favor. He couldn't care though. At that moment, he solely focused on keeping Willa safe.

Safe! Had Mrs. Fremont been able to leave Willa to arrange for anyone to guard her doors? He raced out of the hotel with a startled Bert yelling, "What's your hurry?"

As he ran Mathers' wall-eyed white dog yipped at his heels. Usually, he told it to leave him alone. Today he ignored the animal.

About to run past his store, he stopped instead. No better time to be armed than right now. Entering, he found a gaggle of women surrounding the counter. All chatter ceased when he stepped inside and Mrs. Potter's face glowed with relief when she caught sight of him. "Oh Mr. Dean, you're back. That must mean dear Mrs. Dean will be okay."

He shook my head. "I'm not really back. Just picking up my shotgun to protect her." At those words a collective gasp burst from the women. "Willa will mend, according to the widow. We have her poisoner locked in a room at the hotel." Grabbing the gun that she handed him from where she stood behind the counter, he cracked it to be sure he had left it loaded. "I'll need the extra shells too, Ma'am."

A second gasp escaped from the group after he said that. "Now, don't worry ladies. I'm not starting a war. With that red-headed attacker still on the loose, I want to be prepared."

Looking in Mrs. Potter's direction he said, "I think it'd be best if I locked the store." At her nod, he directed a question to the group, "Anyone have an urgent item she needs to purchase." When no one spoke up, Darrell thanked Mrs. Potter again and looked pointedly at the door. The ladies filed out with him behind them, securing the door.

Gun in hand, he left at a fast clip. Since he carried the shotgun, he didn't run this time which caused the dog waiting outside the store for him to lose interest. Instead, Darrell walked quickly. Leary must have seen him through a window because, as he passed the telegraph office, the detective fell into step beside him.

Without slowing or looking at him Darrell muttered in a low voice, "Suddenly got a terrible feeling about Willa being in danger."

The man grunted. "Had a wire just now that a couple Rangers were down in Granger. They'll be here on today's train."

When they neared Mrs. Fremont's home, Darrell's dread grew as he recognized that her front door stood open. Not something a person did in Colorado during February.

Leary grabbed onto his arm when he noticed that door. "Don't go rushing in there. Remember that window in the bedroom." At Darrell's nod he continued in a voice more gravelly than usual. "You go around there. If that red-haired son of a she-devil is in the room," here he stooped and picked up a large rock, "throw this through the glass and take a shot."

Before Darrell left him, Leary grabbed his arm again. "Give me that gun. Its scatter might harm your woman." He leaned the shotgun against a nearby porch. "Take this colt," he told him as he handed over one of the two matching guns from his holster.

When they heard a scream for help from the direction of the widow's home, he made as if to run. Leary cautioned, "Slow down and do this right. No use anyone except scum getting killed today."

Nodding and filling his lungs deeply to calm himself, Darrell left him and ghosted his way to the bedroom window while Leary headed for the front door. The train whistle sounding in the background promised help, if only the rangers knew where they were.

CHAPTER 10

Help! Her mind screamed it even as she came awake. An older woman who seemed vaguely familiar laid a comforting hand on Willa's shoulder and crooned, "There now dearie! Just lay back and stay still. You've had quite a day."

Memories of bitter drinks, tea, and of an even more vile unknown liquid went through her foggy mind. She remembered vomiting but thought Darrell had been with her. "My husband," she croaked out, desperately wanting him there.

The woman made a clucking sound with her tongue. "He'll be back. Stayed with you during the worst of it and had to go see to your safety."

Her strength gone Willa fell back onto the narrow bed. She wanted to tell the woman how grateful she was for her care. It would have to wait she thought, drifting back to sleep.

It seemed only minutes later that a sharp knock on a door woke her. A voice yelled, "What are you--" before it stopped abruptly. Then she heard stomping and the noise of doors being thrown open. Even with her befuddled brain, she sensed the need to hide.

Unable to summon enough energy to rise, she rolled instead and landed with a thump. Cringing, she hoped whoever searched the house hadn't heard her land on the floor. Spying a nearby armoire placed at an angle in the corner, Willa grabbed a blanket and dragged her body toward it. Knowing she couldn't open its doors while lying on the floor she inched her way behind it, thankful that the piece of furniture didn't sit flush against the wall.

During this she heard a cry for help and expected that to distract the intruder. After that came a sort of pop before the thud of something or someone hitting the floor came and the search continued.

Hidden in the corner, she curled into a tight ball and hid under the blanket. A bit she'd read in The Odyssey came back to her foggy mind then, strangely enough. She remembered reading about Odysseus, exhausted from battling to reach shore, sleeping covered with leaves. These circumstances reminded her of that.

Fear kept her from drifting back to sleep. Willa prayed, asking God to let anyone who looked behind the armoire in the dark room see only an untidy pile of blankets. As her mind formed that prayer, her ears picked up on close footfalls. The intruder had reached this room.

Hearing cursing, she recognized that the intruder was a man. More than that, he said enough vile words for her to realize the attacker from the previous day had found her.

Miss Blackthorn educated her in deportment and self-control. That control kept her from whimpering as what she thought might be the bed crashed against the armoire. As he raged and cursed, she hoped her own emotional control would prove to be an advantage over him.

Hearing retreating footsteps, relief swamped her. He was leaving!

This relief was short lived as the heavy footsteps returned and stopped just in front of the armoire. A scraping noise made her think that he moved the bed away from the armoire. She imagined him opening the doors and heard him curse as he rummaged through it. Lying near the back of the piece, the frightened woman picked up on the noises he made as he moved things around in it.

When those sounds stopped, she knew he had finished searching it. Maybe he'd leave now. Just as she started a prayer begging for him to do just that, the armoire was pushed over and a foot caught her in the ribs.

He found her.

With a tug, the blanket flew and the man roughly yanked her to her feet. Even though fear coursed through her body, she hung like a rag doll as he held her up painfully by an arm. Still, Willa refused to whimper or cry out.

"Look what I found! A pretty little rabbit ready to be shot." He guffawed at his remark, as if he believed it to be a clever joke. She dangled silently from his hand, probably very similar to the rabbit he mentioned.

Fear and the poison she'd ingested earlier that day made her nauseous. His fetid breath added to that as he rumbled, "Wish I had time to do more than just choke you. Always been partial to strawberry blondes." With his free hand, he caressed her breast and she started to heave.

Those dry heaves startled him, so he dropped her onto the floor with a snarled oath. She tried crawling away from him and he kicked her in the head before snatching her up by the arm again. Feeling warmth trickle down her face, Willa inwardly sobbed. She knew she must be bleeding from the blow his boot delivered to her head.

He pulled her against his face and thundered, "I'll be glad to tell Young that you're dead." Then he released her arm and she collapsed onto the floor.

In her hazy mind, Willa heard boots stomp into the room and recognized a second familiar voice. Murphy. Though the man was never friendly she still croaked out, "Thank God you're here."

Willa watched Murphy's face twist into a look of disgust. "Why haven't you killed her yet, O'Hara? I thought Young sent you 'cuz you're good at murder. Geez."

At her whimper, Murphy sneered, "Thought I'd save you huh?" Then he turned to the man she now had a name for and laughed, "It didn't take me long to silence that old crow, Fremont, for good. Do I need to do this one too?" The coldness in that laugh as he spoke about murdering the widow created a terror in her even O'Hara didn't manage to produce.

Murphy pointed a colt at her head, leaving her in no doubt about the way the widow met her end. Tears flowed down her cheeks now and she bit back a whimper. She closed her eyes and waited for the pain.

"Wait! I'm doing this one. You just back off."

Willa's eyes snapped open at that. Looking up, she watched him that familiar length of chain between his fists. As he slowly lowered it toward her, a sudden crash startled them both. A rock flew past her into the room followed by a shower of glass.

"You two better back away from her or you're dead where you stand." Painfully, she turned her head toward the broken window. Joy made its way through her, replacing the cold terror. Darrell was there, pointing a revolver into the room.

O'Hara dropped the chain before taking a step back with his hands in the air. Murphy, however, raised his gun quickly and just as rapidly dropped to the ground.

Shocked, she recognized the Pinkerton shadowed in the doorway holding a still smoking gun. Had she not been so well-trained, Willa might have cried out. Instead she whispered, "Thank God" before the world went black.

The next thing she knew, Darrell shook her shoulder and she woke up in their bed. "Have I been dreaming?" she asked groggily.

He chuckled ruefully. "No sweetheart. You're safe." Leaning down, he gently kissed her forehead before explaining, "I'm sorry to wake you. With that head wound, I have to check you every few hours. We don't want you slipping into such a deep sleep you never come back to me."

Smiling weakly, she assured him, "I'd never want to leave the man I love. Go ahead and wake me up."

This time, he placed a soft, brief kiss on her lips. "You're my whole life. Who would have thought that in less than a month I'd come to love you with my whole being?"

Warmth from his words filled her. She slipped back to sleep knowing she was home.

EPILOGUE

In the end, the two rangers who arrived by train that day had very little to do. They investigated the situation and left without any prisoners. Leary took custody of Rhoda instead.

Rather than put Willa's aunt on trial, Leary transported her by train back to New York. There she became the newest, and hopefully very permanent, resident of the Willard Asylum for the Chronic Insane.

The town turned out for the burial of Mrs. Fremont. In contrast, Murphy was given no funeral. A smart business woman who valued the community's favor, Marie didn't protest when her father's body was taken out and burned.

A month slipped by before Willa and Darrell met Leary again. During that time, the impressive

Miss Blackthorn arrived by train. Like a mother hen protecting her chick, she wanted to see for herself that Willa had survived the ordeal and flourished in her marriage.

Though she only stayed a week she soaked up frontier life like a sponge, continually commenting on things she found admirable about the spirit of the people living in Silver Town. They were, as she put it, "made of sturdy stuff."

While she stayed with them, they received word that Willa's grandfather died. After that, Willa's former guardian shared what she knew of Willa's history. Now that Willa was an adult, Miss Blackthorn reasoned that it was time for her know about her parents.

She told about a carriage accident. "The axle of the vehicle was intentionally damaged, but no one knows who did it or why. Mr. VanDurring died instantly. His wife lingered on." She patted Willa's hand and pride glowed in her eyes when she saw that Willa didn't outwardly show grief at her words.

"You were born soon after, I'm told. Small and determined to live. The only other thing I know is that you were brought to me with a broken arm when you were four." That information didn't surprise them.

Mr. Barrett sent a telegram soon after Willa's poisoning revealing her grandfather hid her away from his daughter because she had abused her niece. According to Barrett, Rhoda VanDurring had been carefully watched by a companion until her father's health failed. As he neared his end, the man decided to institutionalize her. Since he would soon die, he no longer feared the embarrassment this would cause. When she learned of his plans, his daughter disappeared.

The biggest surprise after the arrest of the red-haired man came from Harv Perkins. The evening of Murphy's death, a knock on the alley-side door startled Darrell. The fact that Harv stood on the other side of the door to apologize came as an even greater shock.

"It was Big Murph's idea. I really love Marie, and Murphy pushed me to gain control of the Silver Queen. Said he wanted the mine himself so we made a deal. Murphy talked me into finding a proxy bride for you, just after you got engaged to Marie, back in December. I copied your signature from a document on file at the bank and dated the letter back to the time you were injured, earlier in the year."

Stunned, Darrell didn't say anything immediately. Harv stood in front of him and fidgeted from one foot to the other.

Since he seemed to be in the mood to confess, he decided to ask questions. Fixing the red-faced man with a thoughtful gaze, Darrell tapped a finger to my lips and asked, "I'd really like to know, were any of the lawyers in New York part of this scheme?"

With a nod he answered the question, "Yeah. Horace Young Junior's been my friend since our boyhoods. I sent the letter to him and he agreed to find someone." With a strangled groan he went on, "I didn't know 'bout plans to kill anyone though."

Perkins paused and looked at his feet before meeting his former adversary's gaze. Chagrin filled his face as he continued with his confession, "How could I know he and your wife's aunt would use it to lure her away from her school? I never expected my friend to be part of a murder plot. Not even when I helped Murphy hide the man Young sent here to kill her."

Taking a white handkerchief from his pocket, he wiped at the sweat gathering on his forehead and then nervously twisted the cloth in his hands. "I'm not sure how Barrett knew about the proxy letter. Probably Young's doing. Anyhow, I'm just glad you and your proxy bride hit it off."

Hearing that this man was part of hiding the red-haired assassin caused Darrell to clench his fists. The man was an idiot! He willed himself to relax his fists.

One thing still bothered Darrell. "But how did Albert Crowley get involved?" That was the one final piece of the puzzle he didn't understand. The telegraph operator barely escaped being arrested by the Colorado Rangers. Receiving a stern rebuke, one of the rangers warned that they would be watching him.

Running a hand through his pomaded hair Harv sighed, "Murphy agreed to forgive Crowley's bar tab if he stopped your telegrams and held onto any wires you received." At least now he understood the series of events that brought him the love of his life. He would probably never be friends with this man. Still, he couldn't wish the him any harm. The man seemed to do a good job of bringing disaster to his own life.

"You should be glad those rangers didn't arrest you." Darrell shoved the man back out the door and locked it. Turning to the bedroom, he began the tough work of forgiving Harv Perkins.

One day, about a month after Willa survived both poisoning and the attack, a man walked into the shop. "Thought I'd stop to check on the missus since I'm in town on business."

Looking up, Darrell greeted Leary and asked what brought him back. He harrumphed and wouldn't tell him. Nothing stayed a secret long in Silver Town, though. Not much time passed before Marie Perkins told him the reason for Leary's visit.

While she shopped one day, she said her husband hired the Pinkerton to find his partner in the Silver Queen. He told Leary to force his partner to sign away all rights to the mine in exchange for not being prosecuted. Marie had grown considerably less hostile toward Willa and him in the last few weeks. He expected it might the happiness she found in her marriage. Darrell had heard female customers comment on the attentiveness of Marie's husband. Also, it could be that she was just too busy running the saloon to give them a hard time.

Remembering all of this, he stood deep in thought so that the bell over the door startled him. Looking up, a shame-faced Albert Crowley stood just inside the store. "Thought I'd better bring this wire as soon as I got it." Thrusting it at Darrell, he hustled out without even waiting for a tip.

Mr. Barrett sent the telegram to inform them of Mr. Young Junior's embezzlement. The man had been arrested soon after O'Hara, the red-haired thug, confessed. According to the would-be murderer, Young and Rhoda conspired together to have him kill Willa. Ledgers the lawyer kept revealed he had skimmed thousands of dollars over the years from the VanDurring accounts.

No one knew if he shared any of the money with Rhoda, but Barrett assured them confidently that Young Senior knew about his son's misdeeds. As that man was considered too frail to arrest, authorities filed no charges against him.

Even with the embezzlement, Willa still inherited a considerable fortune. Soon, they would need to make decisions about handling it. For now, New York seemed far away and easily forgotten.

They also needed to consider when they would leave Silver Town, whose population dwindled daily now that the mine remained closed. Darrell's store no longer had enough customers to keep it going.

He should feel burdened by these concerns. Instead Darrell's once stoic face wore a continual smile. Deciding to close early that day, he put a sign in the window and climbed the stairs to enjoy being married to the bride he never sent for.

Willa let out a gasp of surprise when he opened the door then relaxed at seeing him. Before she could ask him why he had closed up already, Darrell swept her up into strong arms and moved to the bedroom.

As he walked, she whispered a secret into his ear. He slowly lowered her so that she once again stood but kept his arms around her. Then he kissed her with all of the passion, thanks, and love that she created in him.

No matter where he decided to move them, Willa and now this baby were his home. Though she had been his fake proxy bride, Willa was his true love.

LEAVE A REVIEW

The End

If you enjoyed this story, I would appreciate it if you would leave a review, as it helps me reach new readers and continue to write stories that appeal to you.

Leave a review at the Amazon page below.

https://www.amazon.com/Bride-Darrell-Proxy-Brides-ebook/dp/B07QJ79GZF

HART'S LONGING

Secrets in Idyll Wood #1

Chapter 1

1887, Idyll Wood, Wisconsin

Why is he here?

Zelly Fuller felt red creep into her face as she caught sight of Ephraim Strong, or Ram as most people called him. This was her best friend's wedding, a special day for both Zelly and her friend Rebecca. They had planned this event together and giggled over for the last three months. Ram should not be a part of this day.

Ram Strong! The name disgusted her. The man disgusted her.

She hid her anger and sashayed to that man's side. He stood with his brother and Ralph Stinson, all three snickering and sneaking sips out of what they kept in their coat pockets.

Stopping in front of Ram, Zelly smiled sweetly. She might not be very experienced with men, but even she knew you get more flies with honey than vinegar.

"Ram, can I speak with you a moment?"

He seemed shocked for a moment. She knew this was probably because she was known as an extremely shy person. The shock quickly left his face, though, and he grinned. "What you want to say Zilly Zelly?"

She almost lost her smile at his use of that hated nickname. At least he didn't complete the taunt he often spouted. Determined to follow through with her quickly formed plan, she fixed an even brighter smile on her face by imagining what she was about to do to the bully.

"No, not here. Won't you stroll with me outside? You know, under that big full moon." Heaven help her, she even batted her eyelashes at him.

"Sorry boys, but the lady needs me." Ram emphasized the word need and the two twits who stood with him guffawed. She wasn't sure exactly why this was funny. She suspected it had something to do with the talk about boys that Mrs. Hoffman, Rebecca's mother, gave her soon after Zelly started developing a figure.

Ram offered her his arm. She hesitated to touch him. Still she needed to keep him off guard if her plan was to succeed so she looped her arm around his.

They walked to the open door of the Hoffmans' hay barn. Mr. Hoffman swept it clean to be used for the reception, with the hay moved outside and covered by tarps to clear a place for the party. Lanterns hung from the bottom side of what was the hay loft in the large barn, giving off a warm butter yellow glow.

The wooden tables now cleared of dishes from the wedding supper were pushed to one side of the barn. Musicians and a dance floor occupied the other side. Before leaving the barn, she looked toward the dance floor and caught sight of the bride. Instead of standing with her groom, Rebecca was speaking with Hart Bahr. As if feeling Zelly's glance, he stared at her.

Nothing new there. He's always staring.

As the Hoffmans' boarder for almost ten years, they considered Hart a member of their family now. She'd shared a supper table with Hart the few times her mother had allowed her to eat at the Hoffmans. Each time was the same. Hart had stared.

Ram felt her pause and looked down at her with an eyebrow raised. "Thought you wanted to *talk* in the moonlight?" His question dripped innuendo, even to Zelly's innocent ears.

She looked up at him in the lantern light, ensuring he was able to see her smile. "Oh yes, please!" she said with a sultry voice. Even if she didn't understand his innuendo, she could easily imitate it.

Holding up the skirt of her light blue dress with her free hand so as not to stain it in the grass, she walked with Ram along the edge of the field that bordered the barnyard. Once they were a short distance away from the celebration, they stopped under an oak.

The scoundrel had made her miserable often in school. She hated him after all of his nastiness through the years.

Suddenly, she remembered a particularly nasty moment when Ram had tried to put a horse apple down the back of her dress. It brought the leaden weight of dread now to her chest. It had been that first year of school. She wore a new dress that her mother, Ma'am, had sewn for her that week, a rare happening, and she'd worn it proudly that day.

While Ralph Stinson distracted her by telling her what a nice dress she had, Ram stood behind her and pulled at the back of her collar, intending to put the smelly horse apple down her dress. When she felt his hand on her she had whirled, ripping her collar. What a whipping she'd received that night!

The memory gave her the strength to act. She looked at him and spoke sweetly. "There's something I've longed to do every time I'm near you."

He leaned into her. "Yeah, well go ahead," he encourage.

Taking her arm away from his and balling her fist, she pulled an arm back to send a punch.

He cursed and put his hand up to stop the fist he saw coming his way. She let out a gasp of pain and tried to pull away.

"Silly Zilly Zelly Fuller." He laughed at her, "Do you remember when I would say 'Zilly Zelly Fuller, what are you full of today?' Well, looks like Zilly

Zelly the mouse is full of courage."

With a quick movement, he pushed her back against the oak tree. Still squeezing her fist with his right hand, he moved his left toward her bodice. She squeezed her eyes tightly shut.

"Zelly, Rebecca's looking for you inside."

Hart waited behind Ram. The pressure on her hand eased and she pulled the hand away from Ram. She quickly skittered around him and ran to join the reception again.

Seeing her immediately, Rebecca waved her over. "Now that Zelly's here, I can toss my bouquet."

"Girls, are you ready?" At Rebecca's question, she forced her mind back to the bouquet of light pink roses Rebecca held high above the crowd as she stood on a chair.

David Hildreth, Rebecca's groom, steadied her as he gazed up at her lovingly. Her friend had everything that she longed for in life.

Still Zelly did not feel jealousy. She loved Rebecca too much to be jealous of her, especially on her friend's special day. No, instead she selfishly considered the change this wedding brought to her own life.

Not quite two years older than her, Rebecca served as her older sister, confidante, and protector. Tonight Zelly tried to stand up to a bully on her own for the first time. Just consider how well that had turned out!

Who will be left in Idyll Wood to care about me after Rebecca leaves?

"Here it comes." Rebecca smiled at Zelly and winked before she threw her bouquet. The flowers flew through the arm and straight into Zelly's hands. Rebecca was playing favorites and had sent it her way, but after all what else should a best friend do?

Knowing how much Zelly longed for a husband and a way out of the home she shared with Ma'am (as Zelly's mother insisted she call her), Rebecca directed the bouquet straight to her. Wanting a good future for her friend, it was no wonder Rebecca tried to send a little luck her way through this old wedding tradition.

Like a champion, Zelly raised the bouquet of beautiful pink roses into the air. The flowers were tied together with a delicate white linen handkerchief. "Hurray!" she exclaimed.

Rebecca threw back her head and laughed as her groom, David, pushed her dark hair behind her ear and whispered something into it. Rebecca threw her arms around David's neck and kissed him right on his lips! What a sight for the young ladies who had gathered to catch the bouquet!

She had to look away, the kiss creating such a longing in her. Romance wasn't what she had on her mind though as she eyed the gathered crowd. She was afraid that Ram might appear. Who knew what form his revenge might take?

Now that the bouquet had been tossed, she decided the party was over for her. Over without even one dance at the wedding!

With a sigh, she sat down, placing the bouquet on the table. There was no way she would ever be married. Why should she keep the silly bouquet that supposedly promised her a future as the next bride who would marry?

"Well, Zilly Zelly Fuller. How should I punish you? Maybe a horse apple down that dress?" She looked up into Ram's menacing face.

She watched his lip curl into a sneer as he tossed out the threat. Rebecca, standing not too far away from the table, quickly made her way to her side.

"Certainly you've outgrown school house pranks Ram! Zelly and I have."

Rebecca whispered for her to stand and then put a hand on her arm. She pulled her across the room towards the sawdust covered dance floor.

Oh, how embarrassing! Is Rebecca going to dance with me since no one else has?

Not able to resist, she looked over her shoulder to see Ram's reaction. The look on his face promised violence.

"Stay away from Ram. He worries me since David and I will be so many miles away from you." At Rebecca's comments, Zelly sighed and hugged her friend. Even at her own wedding, her friend was mothering her.

"He's so handsome Rebecca. He can have any girl he wants. I certainly am not chasing after him." As if she would ever do such a thing!

"I tried to punch him. That's why I went outside with him."

"It didn't work, did it? Men are stronger." Rebecca sighed and shook her head. "Just don't be around him. With as much as your mother makes you stay home, that shouldn't be too hard."

Then they were off. Rebecca dragged her to where Hart stood at the edge of the dance floor. She realized Rebecca was making sure she kept her promise to waltz at least once at the wedding.

She knew she should be delighted to dance with a decent man like Hart. His shoulders filled his brown suit out nicely and, with his dark golden hair and green eyes, she thought he was actually quite handsome.

Three years older than her, he had come to town to attend high school since he could go no further than eighth grade in the country school nearest to his family. He boarded with the Hoffmans and still lived with them, even though he had graduated some years ago.

After merely darting a glance up at him, she quickly lowered her eyes and tucked her chin in an attempt to hide. *Why was Rebecca doing this?*

She wished herself in a darkened corner of the barn. Better yet, she longed to escape the barn, leaving behind this awkward dance and Ram's threats.

Why do I hear Ma'am's words in my head every time I want to speak to a man?

With her eyes downcast and her mother's words *worthless* echoing in her head, she kept her gaze fixed on the floor and felt rather than saw Hart leading her out onto the dance floor for the waltz that was starting.

Did he hold her a bit too close? She rarely danced, and usually just with Rebecca. Perhaps she just wasn't used to being held. That could be why Hart's touch felt overly familiar.

His arm around her waist and the hand holding hers seemed to channel heat from his body into hers as if lightning was moving through him and into her. What an odd sensation!

"Zelly, will you look at me? Won't you give your dance partner one of your sweet smiles?" Hart's voice was gentle, as if coaxing a wild animal to come near to him.

For his trouble, she quickly looked up and flashed a ghost of a smile. It was barely illuminated in the soft light from the lanterns.

She didn't really know him. They shared meals at Rebecca's house, though rarely during the last three months. After Rebecca announced her engagement, Ma'am tightened her hold on Zelly. She seldom allowed her to leave the house now.

The one exception was Sunday. She was allowed to attend church and had even sat next to him in a pew with the Hoffmans. She rarely made conversation with him, though.

Really, she had been too busy talking with Rebecca to spend much time with him. Now she had no idea what to say to him. This awkwardness brought to mind how she felt the many times she caught him watching her.

"With Rebecca moving to Cashton, you'll need a friend Zelly. Can I be that friend?"

At his question, she lifted her face. She wanted to see his green eyes to be sure he was sincere.

Nodding in response to Hart's question, she knew she had a stunned look on her face. Hart smiled broadly, showing his even and white teeth.

His smile produced a flow of happiness in her. She loved pleasing people. Having someone want to please her in return seemed impossible and wonderful at the same time.

She had been sure Rebecca would be her only friend. Ma'am was diligent in telling Zelly how odd it was for Rebecca to accept Zelly as a person and as a friend.

Opening her mouth to thank Hart, quite suddenly, she was stopped by the tight grip on her upper arm.

"Zelly! I said no more than three hours. You certainly had enough time to get into trouble."

With eyes bulging and spittle punctuating each word, Ada Fuller squeezed her arm. "Just like I thought, here I find you with a man!" Zelly winced as those talon-like fingers pinched the flesh of her small arm.

For a very brief moment, Hart's arms tightened around her, as if he wanted to keep her. The moment quickly passed and he dropped his arms away from her.

The fleeting look in Hart's eyes made Zelly wonder if he felt actual regret when he pulled away from her. His look gave her a warm feeling inside and she felt almost valuable.

Now, however, she had no time to think about that. Ma'am dragged her toward the edge of the dance floor. "Please Ma'am. Let me say goodbye to Rebecca and her new husband. I'll just be…"

Ma'am gave a sort of growl in response. The few remaining dancers, who hadn't already halted at the scene Ma'am created, stopped abruptly.

Hart followed after them, asking permission to see them both home. The woman didn't spare a glance in Hart's direction or respond to him.

Zelly's gaze met Mrs. Hoffman's. She hurried forward with a conciliatory look on her face. "Ada, I didn't think you would make it to celebrate with us. Please, let me fetch you a piece of…"

Ma'am neither stopped nor responded, but that didn't surprise Zelly. She honestly believed that Ma'am hated the entire human race.

Before leaving the barn, Zelly managed a hesitant glance over her shoulder to assure herself that Ram hadn't seen. With her last look through the door, she caught sight of the nasty man staring after her. He'd thrown his head backward, laughing uproariously.

Ma'am's actions had merely frightened her. Her enemy's expression, however, brought on a storm of tears.

To Hart, it seemed like a week of silence passed before the musicians began to play again. Couples moved back onto the dance floor.

Though he saw several people shake their heads in disapproval, he didn't believe that anyone was shocked by Ada Fuller's antisocial behavior. After all, everyone in Idyll Wood knew she was a cross old stick.

Hart watched David comfort Rebecca. He, however, stood alone and bereft, gazing out the barn door into the night. Even though he was upset, he still had a difficult time not staring at Zelly's sweet back end as her mother pulled her out into the field they needed to cross.

Finally, he knew what it was like to touch her. Zelly had been in his arms. Having her pulled away from him produced actual pain.

For the last five years at least, he had been keenly aware of her. He watched Zelly during her visits and listened to her stand up for Rebecca when the Hoffman boys teased her. He loved that she was so loyal.

She must be loyal to stay with her witch of a mother.

How can I help her? His hopes for a wife and family were centered, illogically, around that poor broken girl.

He walked to Rebecca's side and placed a comforting hand on her arm. "Don't be afraid for her, Rebecca. She won't be alone after you leave."

Releasing a combined sob and sigh, she shook her head. "What will happen to her? She'll be trapped forever in that house?"

With that, she laid her head onto David's shoulder. Her face showed weariness from the horrendous scene and the excitement of the wedding day.

But he didn't share her discouragement. "Rebecca, your leaving might be the best thing. Without you in town, I'll get a chance to get closer to Zelly.

"But Hart, she won't leave that wicked mother of hers. It's like she holds some secret over her."

Hart smiled. He thought his smile probably made no sense to her. Still he was hopeful.

"Some secrets just have to come out for things to get better." He felt anticipation at finding out Zelly's secret and freeing her.

Seeing the forgotten bouquet on a nearby table, he picked it up and fingered one of the roses absently. "Your parents might not agree with me, but I think it's time for some of Idyll Wood's dark secrets to be revealed."

Read HART'S LONGING now.

Available in Kindle Unlimited.

https://www.amazon.com/dp/B07HHMZT4Z

About Marisa

Marisa Masterson and her husband of thirty years reside in Saginaw, Michigan. They have two grown children, one son-in-law, and two old and lazy dogs.

She is a retired high school English teacher and oversaw a high school writing center in partnership with the local university. In addition, she is a National Writing Project fellow.

Focusing on her home state of Wisconsin, she writes sweet historical romance. Growing up, she loved hearing stories about her family pioneering in that state. Those stories, in part, are what inspired her to begin writing.

Find her on Facebook, in the Chat Sip and Read Community or on her Facebook page.

If you like this book, please take a few minutes to leave a review now! Marisa appreciates it and you may help a reader find their next favorite book!

ACKNOWLEDGMENTS

I want to thank Cyndi Raye, and Charlene Raddon for their ever-present support. A big shout-out goes to Virginia McKevitt for the beautiful cover and to Christine Sterling Bortner for her support and formatting talents.

Some who read this book may recognize that Silver Town actually started out, in my mind, as Creede, Colorado. I didn't feel I could recreate that town adequately in my book so it became Silver Town. Still, I relied on the following for historical information about Colorado and the area around Creede and want to acknowledge them.

https://coloradoencyclopedia.org/article/creede-railroad-depotmuseum

https://www.creede.com/discover-creede/history.html

http://legacy.lib.utexas.edu/maps/topo/indexes/txu-pclmaps-topo-co_nm-index-1928.jpg

A BRIDE FOR DARRELL

This book is a work of fiction. The names, characters, places, and incidents are all products of the author's imagination and are not to be construed as real. Any resemblances to persons, organizations, events, or locales are entirely coincidental.

The book contains material protected under International and Federal Copyright Laws and Treaties. All rights are reserved with the exceptions of quotes used in reviews. No part of this book may be reproduced or transmitted in any form or by any means, electronic or mechanical, including photocopying, recording, or by any information storage system without express written permission from the author.

Scriptures quoted from the King James Holy Bible.